15

Limerock

Maine Stories

▬▬▬

Christopher Fahy

Christopher Fahy

TO NOAH —

BEST WISHES FROM

THE HEART OF MAINE —

Chris , FEB 2000

Coastwise Press
Thomaston, Maine

To Greg and Ben

almost natives

Coastwise Press • 56 Green Street • Thomaston ME 04861

Some of these stories originally appeared
in *New Maine Writing, The Fiction Review,* and *Puckerbrush Review.*

Library of Congress Catalog Card Number: 99-75178

Limerock
stories / by Christopher Fahy

ISBN 0-9626857-5-5

Book and cover design: Carol Inouye, Inkstone Communication Designs
Cover photograph: Neal Parent

Printed in the USA
by Morris Publishing, 3212 E Hwy 30, Kearney NE 68847, 800-650-7888

10 9 8 7 6 5 4 3 2 1

Contents

The Smell of Spring

In the spring Jim was working for summer people: lawyers, both of them, not yet thirty, who'd bought an old wreck of a row house in back of the art museum. Jim and his helper, Kenny, had torn out three first floor partitions, a stairway, had run a steel carrying beam from party wall to party wall in the living room and were putting things back together again when his sister called:

"Gramp's wicked sick. He can't last much longer, the doctor says."

So Jim told the lawyers he needed to go to Maine for a couple of days. Kenny would keep on working while he was gone. The lawyers tried not to look concerned, but they had to be out of their present quarters by June fifteenth.

"We'll make it," Jim said with an audible drag on his cigarette. "Don't worry."

"Okay, if you say so," the male lawyer said. He was wearing a blue oxford button-down shirt and a red bowtie.

"We've never been to Maine this time of year," the female lawyer said. When she smiled, her dark gums showed. "It's probably still winter there."

"Still winter," Jim said.

∼

He took Delta from Philly to Boston, and Coastal the rest of the way. Looking down at the evergreen landscape he saw that the ice had gone out of the lakes. No leaves on the maples yet, just a tentative touch of red at the tips of their branches. In Philly the cherries and tulips had bloomed and the lilacs were budding.

He wished the trouble with gramp hadn't happened in April, spring was a hard enough time without something like that. He hated the summers in Philadelphia, hated the sultry heat and grime, but he didn't feel sad, the way he did in the spring. He had lived in Fishtown sixteen years, and still, when the first warm days came down on those alleys and brick row houses, he felt the sharp pull of Maine.

When he got off the plane in Limerock, the air was cold. Diane was there with the same blue Chevy she'd had six years ago. Like her, it was much the worse for wear.

He put his arm across her shoulder and gave her a tentative hug. He loved Diane, but his family wasn't much for displays of affection.

"You're lookin' good," he said as they got in the car.

"Oh sure," she said with her quiet laugh.

Her face was thin and her hair was a brassy color. He figured he probably looked strange to her, too. Six years ago he'd had his own teeth, and his stomach hadn't been sticking out over his belt.

"So how's Sammy and Tank?"

Diane backed up, looking over her shoulder; ground gears as she shifted to first. "Pretty good," she said.

"Tank still with American Sea?"

"Still there. Sammy's over to Martin Engineering now, likes it better than Goodwin's."

"Still weldin'?"

"Still weldin'."

The road to the airport was lined with modular ranch houses, new since the last time Jim was here. He lit a cigarette and said, "So what's the latest?"

"He's wicked bad."

"That goddamn emphysema."

"Yeah."

"I oughta quit these goddamn things."

"Bad heart and diabetes too. He lost a leg last year."

"You wrote it in the Christmas card."

"Oh, right."

"Eighty-three," Jim said, blowing smoke through his nose. "I thought he'd go when Gramma died six years ago. What a tough old bird. That time we flipped the boat and the fishhook got caught in his chest? He was seventy then. Cut the damn thing out all by himself. Never peeped."

"He's a tough one all right," Diane said, turning a corner.

"Where's Elmer's?" Jim said.

"Tore it down. New convenience store comin'."

"Christ, don't it look funny?"

"That's progress," Diane said. She opened her window a little and smoked sailed out. "I was hoping that Cathy might come with the kids," she said.

Jim smoked. "Well, the kids are in school and Cathy works."

"I didn't know that."

"Yeah, works for a sugar company. Office job."

"She like it?"

"She likes it okay."

"The kids must be so grown up."

"Yeah, Lizzy's fourteen and Dick's nine."

"My God but the time goes fast."

"Don't I know it, Diane."

He smoked. She said, "When you comin' back home to stay?"

He looked at the naked trees by the side of the road. "I don't know," he said. "I never believed I'd be gone so long."

"We miss you," Diane said.

∾

Gramp looked dead. He was thin and white and hooked up to wires and tubes. His mouth was open, hollow, dark, and his eyes were closed, their lids pale, veined with blue. A green line spiked on the monitor next to his bed.

"Gramp?" Jim took the old man's withered hand.

No response, so Jim said it again: "Gramp?"

An intake of breath and the pale lids fluttered.

"It's Jimmy. I'm home."

The eyes came open and fixed on him blankly.

"It's Jimmy, Gramp."

The voice was a whisper, wet: "Jimmy."

"Gramp, I've come home to see you."

The pale eyes shone with a silvery brightness. "You're up in your house? On the hill?"

"No, I'm stayin' in town. With Diane."

"Diane."

"Diane, right here, you see her?"

"No." The old man's eyelids closed for a moment, then opened again, looking wetter and brighter. He said, "Can we go fishin' now?"

"Pretty soon," Jim said. "When you're feelin' better."

The wrinkled eyelids closed again; the thin mouth twitched. Jim said, "Hey, remember the time I caught the six pound brownie? Two o'clock in the afternoon. You said we'd never get anything that time of day, then I hooked into that."

No response.

"We were just about ready to quit," Jim said, "but you let me cast one more time and by God did that sucker strike."

Diane touched his arm. "He's gone," she said.

Jim looked at his grandfather's purple lips. When the nurse and intern came rushing in, he turned away and looked outside at the trees.

~

The ground had thawed enough to dig the hole. It was foggy out at the graveyard and foggy at Tank's. There was was plenty of booze, but Jim didn't touch it. He hadn't touched booze since his accident.

Tank was the oldest, seven years older than Jim. His hair was gone except for a fringe in back, and his stomach was huge. He put away plenty of food and booze and talked in a loud rough voice about his job, the buck he'd shot, ice fishing, the prospects for this year's Sox. Sammy, two years younger than Tank, had lost some weight since Jim had last seen him and had a large scar on his cheek. He said to Jim, "You been back to the house?"

"No."

"You plannin' on goin'?"

"I have to take off in the mornin'. I'm doin' a house down there, big townhouse, my God what a wreck it is. Two lawyers. They own a cottage around here somewheres, near Nortonville. You been by my place?"

"Drove by it last week," Sammy said, "Don't look too good."

"It's still standin' at least," Jim said. "In Philly they'd burn it down."

"You still plannin' to fix it?"

"Christ, Sammy, I wish I could, but I been so busy."

"Your family likes it better down there."

"Cathy does. The kids liked it here pretty good the few times they came."

"I hardly remember them. Too bad they couldn'ta got to know Gramp better."

"It's hard to believe he's gone. It's the end of an era."

"You're right, it is."

"He was some kinda man, all the father I ever had."

"You don't even remember Daddy, do you, Jim?"

"Hell no, I was only three when he he had his heart attack."

"Right, I was only eight. It's like yesterday to me, it's still that clear. Still holdin' the axe. Uncle Vic had to pry his fingers off it. Forty-three, imagine that, that's all he was—two years younger than I am now."

"And I'm forty."

"By God, so you are," Sammy said.

Tank's wife, Darlene, put out more food the various nephews and nieces came running to stuff themselves. Jim couldn't remember all their names; some were Colsons and some were Cobbs and some were Mathewsons. Tank said to one of them, one of his boys, "Go fetch that item for Uncle Jim," and the kid ran off. Jim smiled. *Fetch*. You never heard that in Philly.

The boy returned with something Jim thought had been lost to time. Tank drew the tip of the rod from the faded green canvas case and said, "You're the one who should have this, Jim, he'd want you to."

The feel of the rod took him back twenty years. "I caught my big brownie with this," he said.

"What a hell of a fish that was," Tank said. When he laughed, ashes fell from his cigarette. "And don't think Gramp warn't jealous, neither."

The rod was ancient, varnished cane, and the windings around the eyelets had lost their yellow. Jim stared at it, layers of memories rushing up, then slipped it back into its case.

"There's still brownies in Bailey Pond," Tank said. Pollution ain't got 'em all yet. Maybe you'll get down here this summer, show us how it's done."

"Yeah, maybe," Jim said. When they left Tank's place, it was raining.

～

Overnight, the rain became snow. Six inches were on the ground by morning, and still it fell. All flights were cancelled. Shortly after ten o'clock a bright, warm sun broke through and things started to melt. Coastal had a flight at six-fifteen that Jim could catch. Having nothing better to do till then, he borrowed the car from Diane and drove out to the house.

The house had intrigued him as far back as he could remember. On Bailey Pond, fishing with Gramp, he'd stare at its massive square bulk at the top of the hill. "It used to be ours," Gramp said one day, surprising him. "My grandfather's father built it in 1820. He was a sea captain, sailed to Australia and China and India, all kindsa places all over the world. He brought back treasures, got rich, built that house. My grandfather lived there when I was a boy. He died when I was ten years old, and Daddy sold the place to a couple named Hamilton, outtastaters who only came summers to fish and swim in the pond. They're dead. It's been empty for twenty years."

When Jim was in high school a sale sign went up on the house. He drove out alone and climbed through a cellar window. Ten foot high ceilings with plaster moldings, chestnut doors, brown velvet drapes, a sweeping view of the pond from the widow's walk, and east, a glimpse of the bay. He wandered the overgrown orchard and matted fields, and standing beside the quick clear brook, he thought: Gramp came here when he was a boy. This house was ours.

All during his years in the navy—in Norfolk, San Diego, Philly—he thought of the house and saved his money. His mother died halfway through his last hitch, and he came back to Maine for the funeral. The house, amazingly, was still for sale, and he put a down payment on it.

His dream had been to fix it up and raise his family there, but Cathy had hated Maine from the very start. No leaves on the trees in the middle of May, it was cold, everybody talked strange. Nobody had any money and jobs were scarce, and it took a whole day to drive to where her parents and sisters lived. He took her out on the bay and she got so sick he had to carry her back to the car, and a black fly bit her under the eye and her face swelled up like a melon. She swore she'd never move to Maine and begged him to sell the house.

He refused. Someday she'd change her mind, he figured. Someday she'd tire of traffic and crime and crowds.

It hadn't happened, but still he held onto the house. He had only been back to look at it twice in all the years he'd been married. But when he was driving those hot spring streets with the waves coming up from the asphalt, it made him feel good to think of the house and know it was back in Maine hands—in Colson hands—and was waiting for him on that hill looking down at the pond.

The last time he'd seen it, six years ago, he'd found the parlor fireplace filled with ashes, the black slate sink in the kitchen filled with cans. Surely the place would burn someday; his luck couldn't last forever. He knew he should take out insurance, but couldn't afford it; paying the real estate taxes was hard enough.

Diane had written him several years back that she thought he could get at least twice what he'd paid for the house because more and more summer people were buying and driving the prices up. He wouldn't consider selling, though, and Cathy exploded. Here they were, strapped for money, she'd had to go back to work to make ends meet, and still he held onto that horrible wreck in that horrible place, paying those stupid taxes. One night, after one of these arguments over the house he finished a sixpack and found himself driving right into a sweet dream of fishing on Bailey Pond. He woke with the car racked up on a pole, his mouth filled with blood and his front teeth gone.

And now, as he drove down the lonely road past fields holding clots of snow, he thought about Philly. No snow there for over a month. Near eighty a couple of days last week, and soon the little park near his house would be bright with azaleas and dogwoods. He still wasn't used to that April heat, all those sudden lush flowers and leaves. No matter how long he lived down there, it could never be home—as Maine could never be home to Cathy or Lizzy or Dick, or the lawyers whose house he was fixing.

The driveway was soft with thick mud, so he parked on the road and walked. In the stand of white pines that lined the drive, a pair of bluejays darted. You rarely saw jays in Philly. Instead you saw cardinals and Baltimore orioles, southern birds.

Suddenly, there by the eastern wall—by the lilacs that wouldn't bloom for another month—the smell of spring, Maine spring, so different from Philadelphia spring. So clear and clean, with a taste of the ocean in it.

The house was a mess: the floor of the porch had rotted through and the chimneys were falling down. One of the wooden gutters was gone and rain had been pouring into the cellar for quite some time, undermining the stone foundation. The roof was wavy in sections, its shingles cracked. If he was going to fix this place, he'd have to do it soon.

My grandfather's great-grandfather built this house, he thought, the man with the muttonchop whiskers, the captain. He sailed to Asia and brought back treasures, and we join the coast guard and navy and bring back tattoos. He was rich, that old man, where the hell did the money go? Sammy and Tank and Diane and me, we all work hard and don't have a pot to piss in.

He went around back and looked out at the pond, the pond where he used to fish with Gramp, where he caught his huge trout. Along the water's eastern rim he could see four cottages angled among the trees. Six years ago, the last time he'd come— no cottages there. He wondered if Gramp had seen them. He hoped not. The lawyers he worked for had built a place further north, on what they said was an "unspoiled" pond. Jim wondered which pond it was. Most of the ponds he knew were pretty well spoiled, in his opinion.

He looked at the house again, at bright snow melting and dripping along the rotting eaves, and thought: For Christ's sake, who are you kidding?

His wife hated Maine. But he loved her, and loved his kids. And the kids loved the Jersey shore, with suntan lotion, surfboards, friends, not the rocky deserted beaches here, this icy water. He would never come back to Maine, who was he kidding?

∼

As they sat in the airport waiting room, he stared at his mudspattered shoes and then finally he said: "Diane, I'd like you to call Ted Harris and tell him to list the house."

Under the pale fluorescent light, Diane looked older than ever. "Oh, Jimmy," she said.

"Look, maybe when the kids are grown I'll find a camp down here, but the house is too much. And if somebody doesn't get after it soon, it's gonna fall over."

Diane, his baby sister, thirty-eight—and how had the time gone by so fast?—said, "Okay, I'll call Ted Harris."

"Thanks," Jim said. "But get him to promise something."

"What?" Diane said, looking so tired, so old.

"Get him to promise he won't sell the place to no summer people."

The Rock

"I mean most of these dudes here think they can just hang around and wait for the seller to come to *them*," Mr. Markson said.

He was tilted back in his swivel chair, legs crossed, a cigarette held loosely in his tobacco-stained, pudgy hand. He laughed. "They've been doing business that way since Christ was in diapers, it's all they know." He brushed at his shirt, at a crumb or fleck of ash that Oram couldn't see, or perhaps a wrinkle. Oram sat taller, twisting his neck against the constraint of his tie.

The business method that Mr. Markson was laughing at was the business method that Oram had always assumed *he* was going to use. He'd thought that's how real estate worked: you came to the office, sat at your desk, and people phoned in or stopped by. But it wasn't like that. Sitting at your desk—"floor time," it was called—was limited to half a day a week, and when you were new, you didn't get any at all.

"A seller who comes through that door today is here because of *me*," Mr. Markson had said. "For *you* to get that listing would be like a bird laying eggs in another bird's nest. You see my point?" "Yes sir," Oram had said.

Mr. Markson tipped forward now and the swivel chair creaked with his weight. He sucked on his cigarette and said, "There's only one way to make bucks in this racket, Oram, and floor time's not it." Another drag; his mouth went wide; the smoke sat there a second, obscuring his tongue, disappeared, then flowed out through his nose. He ground the butt into the clear glass ashtray, drank some coffee from his mug and said,

"You have to *stalk* your listings, you have to *recruit*. Back home, the guys who couldn't recruit just withered away on the vine."

Oram twisted his neck again. He hated ties. He couldn't seem to breathe right with them on.

Mr. Markson smiled and said, "You're probably thinking, 'It's different in Maine, Maine isn't New Jersey.' Well it isn't—not yet. But it will be, just give it some time. Jersey's ahead of Maine in everything, and real estate's no exception. The people prepared to change right now are the people who'll lead the pack. That's why I hired you, Oram. I think you're willing to try new methods, not get stuck in the same old patterns. Am I right?"

Oram swallowed. "Yes sir," he said.

The office wasn't really hot, but Oram was sweating. This was only his second full day on the job. After three years as gofer at Holcombe's Lumber and another two years at Shop 'N Save, he sure needed something better, employment with some sort of future, and he didn't want to have to move to Massachusetts to get it. The real estate business had seemed like a good idea when his mother suggested it to him, the courses hadn't been too bad, he'd studied hard and passed the test the first time out, but he really wasn't sure about Mr. Markson. Yesterday Markson had told him: "You'll learn pretty fast that your biggest friends in this racket are death and divorce." Oram hadn't liked that much, but no other brokers were hiring now, it was Markson or nothing.

"To make money, you have to sell, and in order to sell, you need listings."

"I realize that, sir. They stressed it in school."

Markson nodded. "Okay, I can send out letters and knock on doors, but you *know* this area, Oram. You know where the good stuff is and who's ready to move it. You know who the FISBOs are."

"FISBO" meant "For Sale by Owner." Oram had learned that yesterday. He said, "I guess so, sir."

~

When he got behind the wheel of his rusty Tempo, Oram thought: Maybe old Mrs. Webb. Joe Perley wouldn't sell his shore lot, he clammed down there, and Harlan Trout raked blueberries on his farm. Harlan had moved to his place in town before Oram was even born and had let the farmhouse and barn run down, but he wouldn't sell. "Where would my pies come from if I didn't hold onto that land?" he'd said, and had made it sound perfectly logical, too. But now that her youngest grandchild, Hank, was grown and gone, Mrs. Webb just might part with her camp.

He found it hard to meet her eyes. She said, "Well, Oram, it's crossed my mind, of course. Nobody's had much use for the place these last few years, it's in pretty sad shape, Milt drove me down last month when the mud dried up. The bedroom roof's leaking some bad, the chimney needs mortar, the door to the privy's gone."

Oram straightened the doily that sat on the arm of the sofa and cleared his throat. "It's a nice spot, Mrs. Webb. Real quiet and pretty, good fishing and swimming, too. I think we could sell it pretty quick. I think we could get forty thousand for it."

Mrs. Webb looked astonished. "Forty thousand! My word, I bought that place for fifty dollars when Helen and Milt were kids. Of course, we added to it some, but forty thousand dollars! Who'd pay that much for a tiny camp with a hundred feet of shore?"

Oram frowned at the fringe on the shade of the lamp, then looked at Mrs. Webb again—but not at her eyes. "Summer people," he said.

The old woman seemed thoughtful. She brushed at a stray white wisp of hair and said, "I suppose you're right. Well, I don't know..." But before another half hour had passed, she'd agreed to sell.

~

It was Oram's only listing for the month. So far, he hadn't made a dime, and his savings were almost gone. Spring was here now, though, and things often improved in the spring. He sure hoped they did, and fast. Mr. Markson was getting upset. He'd said, "For god's sake, Oram, you have to *hustle*. I rounded up six listings, and I don't even *know* these people. You'll have to do better than that if you want to make money. *Think*. Use your *head*."

Oram thought, and another week went by. He consulted his mother, but she wasn't much help. A FISBO sign went up on Maple Street, but year 'round summer people owned that place, not somebody local. Most of the people his family knew held onto their land, passing it down from one generation to the next. Sometimes they'd sell a camp when their kids grew up, or part with an extra shore lot, or if they were really desperate they'd move out of state. But those things didn't happen every day, as Markson seemed to expect.

～

Somebody finally called about Mrs. Webb's camp. It was on a Saturday, and the weather was perfect: sixty degrees, warm for April, with a cloudless, powderblue sky. Oram met the people on route 52, and they followed his Tempo down the dirt lane to the pond. They had a burgundy Volvo with New York plates, a new one, and a thin film of dust dulled its shine by the time they parked. The family—a man and woman, boy and girl—got out and shut the doors.

The man had a trim black beard and thinning hair. Wire-rimmed sunglasses hid his eyes. His pants were a light green plaid and his sportscoat—tan—had a belt that hung from a pair of loops in the back. He tugged at the sportscoat's cuffs then said in a sour voice, "What's the name of this place again?"

"Carver Pond," Oram said.

"And is this a town road?"

"Private road."

"It's in pretty rough shape. The cottage owners pay an equal amount to maintain it?"

Oram started to sweat. He owned two sportscoats, a brown corduroy and a lightweight navy blue cotton, and to his regret he had chosen the corduroy. "I believe they do pay an equal share," he said, "but I'll have to check."

The man looked annoyed. He scuffed at a leaf with the toe of his shiny black shoe. The little girl pulled on the woman's dress and said, "I'm hungry, Mommy."

The woman—light brown hair and a placid smooth face—said, "Be patient, darling, we won't stay long."

"But I'm *hungry*."

"I know, sweetheart. Be a good girl now."

They walked down the path to the camp, which was set at the water's edge. When Oram had come here with Mr. Markson to check things out and put up the sign, the dock had not been in. Now it was, and the boy ran over to it.

"Sweetie, no, hold my hand," the woman said. The boy changed his mind, turned around, ran up to the doorless privy. He stuck his head inside and said, "This *stinks!*"

"Matthew, come back here!" the woman said. The boy tipped up on his toes, peering into the privy's darkness, then returned to the dock.

Oram looked at the pond. A loon skimmed its mirrored surface, dived, was gone and gone and gone, then popped up thirty feet away from where it had disappeared. Near the rock, Oram thought. The rock was completely hidden now, but in August, unless there was plenty of rain, its top would protrude brown and dry, a miniature island. Its top was flat, as if it had been sliced off. You could stand on it with one foot.

Across the water, above the trees, Hatchet Mountain was crisp and blue. A patch of snow still clung to its western slope, and down at its base you could see the brand new condos going up. They were tiny from here, but tiny or not, they looked wrong. Maybe when they got their clapboards and roof shingles on they would blend in better. The loon dived again. Hatchet Mountain's reflection shivered.

"Nice scenery," Oram said. "And it's private, too. There's only ten camps here—or maybe eleven."

Five cottages stood at the water's edge and the rest were hidden. The one on the far right, under the huge white pine, was where Amy had lived. It was still the same forest green color that Oram remembered. "Once the leaves come out, the other camps pretty much disappear too."

"This water's *yukky*," the boy said, jabbing around with a stick he'd discovered and stirring up matted leaves.

You dived, kicked hard, held your hands straight out and counted, One, two, three...till you reached the rock. Eight was the record, and Oram had set it. The closest Hank had come was ten. They had never once gone for a swim without touching the rock, the rock was good luck.

Oram thought of the water's sharp cold on the length of his body, its dark secret taste. He remembered the times on Amy's float: the warm planks sending up cedar smell, how Amy would splash him and scream when he barreled in after her, thrashing. She'd stayed in Maine, was married now, had a child, a girl, and worked at Star Rope, on the floor.

"Good swimming," Oram said. There were leeches sometimes, but he guessed he could leave that out. "Good fishing, too. White perch, black bass, brown trout..."

Frowning, the man said, "My guide to Maine lakes doesn't mention brown trout in here."

"Well they're here," Oram said. "I've caught them here."

The man's teeth showed as he made a sucking sound. "Has the soil been tested for a septic system?"

Oram shrugged. "I doubt it. This pond is pretty old-fashioned. I don't think anyone here has a flush. Half of them don't even have electric. But the water's real clean, you can drink it."

"Drink *this?*" the boy said with disgust as he held up some black rotted leaves on the end of his stick.

The girl whined. "Mommy, I'm *hungry*."

"I know, Samantha," the woman said. "We'll be leaving soon, sweetheart."

Oram went to the screened-in porch. On the floor in there was Hank's baseball bat.

The man said, "We don't need to look inside, we'd tear down the shack. All we're interested in is the lot."

"Oh," Oram said.

"What a yukky house!" the boy said. The woman laughed.

The man's frown deepened. "They want forty thousand."

"That's right," Oram said.

"Well, we'll let you know."

Oram was now supposed to say there were several other interested parties, but somehow he couldn't do it. All he said was, "Okay."

~

The man called late that afternoon, just as Oram was leaving the office. Mr. Markson had said, "Be tough now. Nail him down. You've got to get them early, or they slip off the hook." Then he'd left for the day.

The sour voice said, "The dock's in poor shape, the soil's not tested, the shack itself is hopeless. We also have some doubts about the purity of the water. What we're looking at here is location, so we'll offer twenty thousand."

"Twenty thousand," Oram said.

"That's our offer."

Oram's breath echoed back at him from the phone. "Let me see if I have your number here. 592-8425?"

"That's right, 8425, the Harbor Inn, room 39."

"I'll present your offer to the owner and call you back."

"Soon, I hope."

"Soon as possible, sir."

Oram hung up the phone and sat back in his chair. He stared at the elm tree across the street, at the giant red X on its trunk. There wouldn't be any leaves on that elm this spring, it was dead. Most elm trees were. The X meant they'd take it down.

And rumor said that the old house behind it was coming down too, that McDonald's was going to build a restaurant there.

Oram thought about that. He thought of the condos on Hatchet Mountain, of Amy, of old Mrs. Webb, of Hank.

When five minutes had passed, he dialed the Harbor Inn. "Room 39, please," he said.

When the man got on, Oram said, "Sir, the owner won't sell."

A pause, and then: "She won't accept our offer?"

"She won't accept *any* offer. She's keeping the place."

A scratchy sound. "Well what was the point...? I mean why...?"

"I don't know, sir. I guess she just changed her mind."

"For Christ's sake, that's ridiculous! All right, then, twenty-five thousand."

"I'm sorry, sir, she just won't sell."

"Well is anything else of a similar nature available?"

"I don't know of anything, sir."

The line was silent.

"If I come across anything," Oram said, "I'll let you know."

"We have to go back to New York in the morning. Jesus! Well here's my address..."

≈

Oram stood on the porch of the camp and took off his corduroy jacket. He took off his tie, his shirt, his shoes, his socks, his pants, his underwear. The sun was well below Hatchet Mountain and the air was cool.

Oram had fixed the floor of this porch with Hank five years ago, when they were both seventeen. That fall, Hank had gone off to college in Massachusetts, found good-paying summer jobs down there and had never come back.

Oram opened the screen door, naked, and jogged down the short narrow path. When he reached the dock he broke into a run. The boards thumped hollowly under his feet and then he was flying. The cold hit him hard, with a rush, was silver and painful along his sides as he counted, One, two, three...

He made it to twelve before reaching the rock and burst up gasping for air, his heart loud in his ears. His fingers found the familiar crevice and he hung on, fighting for breath.

He'd been seven years old, was just learning to swim, he had gone out too far while the others were all inside, and he'd started to sink. Kicking and flailing in panic he'd shouted, "Help!" and had choked on a mouthful of water. Then his foot hit the rock, he braced himself on it, the screen door slammed, his father was diving, was there, had his arms around him. From that time on, the rock had been good luck.

Oram's heart slowed down. He looked across at Hatchet Mountain, the condos ringing its base, and thought of Hank. Out loud he said, "I don't want to work in Massachusetts." He looked at the cottage where Amy had lived, at the snow on the mountain's side. The trees were almost black in the dying light. He shouted: "I don't want to work at goddamn Star Rope, either!" His words made a hollow thin echo, dissolved in the trees.

Freezing now, his teeth clicking hard, he leaned on the rock with both hands and counted to eight. Then he planted his feet on its dimpled surface, pushed off, and swam back to the dock.

The Glow of Copper

A slash of light made Hattie Slocum pull over. She shifted to neutral, kept the engine running, and stared at the house that stood on the opposite side of the windblown field.

She spat on her palm and rubbed at a greasy smear on the pickup's window. It didn't budge, so she rolled the window down. The glass wobbled and squeaked.

She was wearing Alfred's heavy shirt, and fastened the highest button against the cold. The shirt wasn't so good anymore. The black checks were black as ever, even blacker, but the white ones were yellow as an old dog's teeth. The bottom two buttons were gone, as well as the ones on the cuffs, and the wool was full of holes from those goddamn rats. She reached through the hole above the left pocket, felt around in her gray work shirt, located a Chesterfield. Sticking the cigarette in her toothless gums, she struck a match and lit up.

Last week of September, and already cold. She had only two cords of wood, that foolish Cubby—

There—on the edge of the eave—she saw it again: that shine, the glint of sun on metal. She squinted. New asphalt shingles. They'd put on a whole new roof—and had flashed it with copper!

The summer people had promised to live there year 'round, not just in season, and they'd kept their word, but look what they'd done to the place! Every time she went by—which was once every couple of months—things had changed. The summer before, they had torn out the bamboo, cut the pucker-brush, put in a big new kitchen window and painted the trim. In the fall, storm windows and doors had gone up, and spring had brought skylights, a new electric service, new clapboards on the south...

And now the roof. Hattie had seen that roof done twice before in her life: once when she was a girl, when Daddy did it with cedar shingles—Uncle Van had helped—and the time she and Alfred did it with asphalt. When? Right after Korea, wasn't it? It had to be, they were back from Bath Iron Works. My God, that long ago. It was due, all right: the open chamber had leaked some bad the last few years, and the ceiling was damn near wrecked.

The cold wind rippled the field, sending waves toward the house. *Good Jesus, copper,* Hattie thought. She and Alfred had flashed it with galvanized sheets from the printer, stuff he was throwing out. They used feed bags under the shingles instead of tarpaper, too. When you didn't have money, you learned to make do. She took a warm drag on her Chesterfield, thinking of Alfred. Oughta quit these filthy things, she thought, but doubted she ever would.

Buddy, her youngest, had asked, "Don't you wanta go in and see what they done to the place? It must be tore up somethin' wicked, they had a mountain of plaster and laths out there." "No," Hattie had answered, "I wanta remember it like it was. Like when me and Oscar and me and your daddy lived there."

Just seeing that garden spot was hard enough, and God only knew what she'd find if she went inside. She and Alfred had grown enough food for a dozen people in that plot: squash and potatoes and turnips and carrots and cabbage enough to last all winter, packed away in leaves down cellar—and now there was a big two car garage standing right where the corn had been! It was built on damn good dirt, they used to shovel out the stable there. Now flowers grew next to the house where the bamboo used to be, but these people didn't grow food. Didn't *have* to grow food.

The pickup wheezed and died. Hattie crushed out her cigarette and turned the key. The engine protested, sputtered, caught. She pumped the gas.

"Hi! How are *you?*"

Hattie jumped. Through the window she saw the rosy, square-jawed face she sometimes saw in dreams. How the hell had she let him sneak up like that, was she losing her mind? She forced a smile. "Well, hi! Pretty cool for September, ain't it?" She felt her pulse speed up.

"Frigid," the man said, blinking. He was wearing a brown felt hat, sort of a derby, and a thick red flannel shirt like they sold at Bean's. It looked brand new.

"Got your wood in?" Hattie asked.

The square-jawed man hesitated a second, then said, "All set."

"You heat with just wood or you use coal too?"

"We use quite a bit of wood, but we put in a furnace. See the chimney?"

Hattie looked at the house again. Two flues. She hadn't noticed that, her eyes must really be going. "Oh, that's good," she said.

"The way wood's escalated in price, you probably don't save much over oil these days."

"I guess that's true," Hattie said, thinking, True if you *buy* your wood. She remembered that time they ran out: she was sick all fall and Alfred was working in Bath and the kids hadn't cut enough for the kind of winter they had. It was gone by the middle of March, and the cold came down real hard. She burned cardboard boxes, she burned an old chair, and then there was nothing left to burn and it dropped to zero inside. She walked up and down the road holding Buddy, the baby, in her arms, till the sun came up. Sick as she was, she walked for hours. It was the only way she could think of to keep Buddy warm.

The man—what the hell was his name?—said, "You have time to stop in?"

Hattie nudged the accelerator, shaking her head. "No, I gotta get home," she said. "Got tons to do around the place."

"Just for a minute? To see how we've fixed things up?"

The engine died again and Hattie thought, *Damn*. This truck had cost her half the money these people had paid for her house, and now it was stalling out. In the silence she felt herself starting to sweat.

"Cackie hasn't seen you in ages," the man said. "She'd love you to visit."

Cackie. Catherine, her real name was, it was on the deed. Cackie was a silly-ass, rich woman's nickname. "I better get back," Hattie said, "my truck's actin' up. I better get Buddy to check it out."

"How *is* Buddy?" the man said brightly. "I saw him at Ace Hardware, oh, about six months ago."

"He's fine," Hattie said, and wondered: Had they seen Buddy's name in the paper last week? Operating under the influence, driving to endanger...

"Why here's Cackie now," the man said.

Good God, she was already halfway across the field. Tall, golden, sleek, and looking like she owned the whole damn world.

The hay was up to her waist. If Hattie still owned the house, that hay would have been cut twice by now, but these people didn't have horses, didn't have animals at all, that's what Luke had said. The barn where her Sally and Toby had lived was used for storage now.

Shielding her eyes with her hand and smiling, Cackie came up to the truck. "Why Hattie, it's *so* good to see you," she said. "But I feel so *guilty*. We've been meaning to have you to dinner for over a *year*. *Impossible* to believe so much time has gone by. Can you join us for lunch?"

Hattie's work pants were splattered with dirt and grease. Straw stuck out of her sleeve. "No, I have to get home," she said.

"Steamed mussels," Cackie said. "Am I tempting you?"

Steamed mussels. Depression food, that's what they used to eat in the days of no money. "Sounds good," she said, "but I gotta go bank that trailer of mine. Won't be long before snow, by the feel of it."

"Well stop in for just a minute, then. You just *have* to see what we've done." She smiled again. "Come on."

Hattie protested again that she had to get back. But the next thing she knew she had opened the pickup's groaning door and was hunching out of the cab and limping along beside Cackie, who said, "We'll walk up the drive, it's easier than going through the field."

The drive had been scraped and leveled and topped with crushed stone. There hadn't been any sinking up to your hupcaps in mud *this* March. "We *love* this field," Cackie said. "In the spring it's just gorgeous, and even now, as dry and brown as it is, Fred and I both think it's terribly attractive."

Fred, that was his name, thank God the woman had mentioned it. "This field fed a lot of animals," Hattie said.

"I imagine it did," Fred said.

The sparkling white chips of stone crunched under Hattie's boots. Must've cost a goddamn arm and a leg to have this laid down, she thought. When she looked at the house again, she thought: It seems bigger, but why? The way the eaves were painted blue, that kind of blue they used in Camden and Wiscasset, maybe that was doing it.

"Do you like our new roof?" Cackie asked.

"Oh yes, it's *elegant.*"

Fred laughed. "I don't know if I'd go *that* far."

"I think the copper flashing really *is* elegant," Cackie said; and looking at Hattie, she added, "We love the glow of copper."

"So don't I!" Hattie said, and thought: The glow of gold ain't hard to take either.

Cackie frowned, but kept smiling. "We wondered why the old roof was done in three colors," she said. "We'd never seen anything quite like that before."

Hattie cackled. "Oh, that was my idea. I said to Alfred, 'We put on a roof that's red, white and green, nobody's ever gonna miss *our* place.'"

"Ah-ha," Fred said. "So that was it."

No, Hattie thought as she limped along, that *wasn't* it. They had bought Ralph Watkinson's leftover shingles cheap, *that* was it. They'd never had enough money to buy all one color.

The wind rolled through the hay again, and Hattie thought of Toby. Nicest horse in the world, that Toby, but he got the heaves. No money for the vet when he first took sick, and after he got the heaves he was finished. He was buried right next to the barn... The barn! She laughed sharply and said, "Will you look at the barn!"

It was covered with cedar shingles. Hard to see from this far away, but they looked like first clears, maybe even selects. First clears or selects on a barn!

Fred said, "What a project. The whole south wall was rotted out, I had to have it totally rebuilt."

"Don't surprise me none," Hattie said. "It was gettin' some bad when I was here. That place is made out of secondhand lumber to start with, you know. Me and Alfred tore apart an old chicken coop up to Slab Hill, hauled it down in a trailer and put up that barn. We lost our good one to lightnin', same way I lost my daddy. You two oughta get lightnin' rods. They say it never strikes the same place twice, but I don't believe it, do you?"

Cackie's smile was broad this time. "No, I don't," she said.

They had reached the house. It wasn't a long walk, really, but Hattie's bum hip—the one she had broken at Star Rope years ago—was throbbing bad. She was sixty-eight, and thought as she caught her breath: It's better to live on the road at my age, not up a dirt drive. Especially in spring, if you can't afford gravel and have to park down at the end and hike in because of the mud. But she missed the place, she really did. When she looked around at all these people had done, her heart ached.

They had torn out the bridal wreath by the door—the one that Suzie had planted when she was a kid—and the lilac that Daddy had planted. It looked funny without them, wrong. They had put in all different things—azaleas, it looked like, laurel, too, and that other plant with dark green leaves that the doctor had around his house, roto-something. All the bamboo was gone. Well, good riddance to that. But of course it wasn't really good riddance, you never wiped out bamboo, no matter how smart or how rich you were. She could see a few of its dark red spears at the base of some laurel. Let it go for a couple of months and they'd have a jungle again.

The catwalk up to the front door was gone, replaced by brick. Not secondhand chimney brick, new paving brick. "I always wanted to do that," Hattie said, "get rid of them boards, but what looked like a little rock under there was a boulder! How'd you move it?"

Fred said, "Weldon Farris bulldozed it out. He's been such a help."

Hattie stared at the bricks and said, "Well, that's nice to hear."

She had lived next to Weldon Farris all her life. When times were rough after Oscar died—back when pulpwood sold so cheap that even if she sawed all day she couldn't make enough to pay her taxes and feed everybody too—Weldon hadn't offered to help. He hadn't offered to help because he wanted the town to take her house so he could buy it cheap. He didn't want the house, he wanted the land—the field and the well. He'd have torn down the house if he'd got it. But he didn't get it: she married Alfred, then the war came along and there was work. Thank God for World War Two. Then three years ago when the house got so rundown she had to move into the trailer, Weldon made her an offer on it. She refused, although she couldn't pay her taxes, then the summer people came along and she sold it to them for less. Weldon had always sucked up to summer people, so it seemed only right that he had them for neighbors now. Anyway, he was an atheist, and he deserved it.

"Shall we go inside?" Cackie said.

Hattie's stomach sank. She limped onto the granite step—they hadn't changed that, at least—and crossed the threshold.

She laughed, though she felt so turned around she was dizzy. The stairs were still in the same spot, right in front of her, but now they were covered with carpet. The bannister was gone, replaced by a wall and a modern railing. Her kitchen was now a dining room with a round oak table and six oak chairs; sun from the picture window fell in a brilliant bar at the foot of the table, right at the edge of the oriental rug. And the brand new kitchen—was in Daddy's room! They had torn down the wall and put the kitchen there!

Feeling slightly sick, she said, "Don't that window look great. It's so *light* in here."

"Opening up that wall has made *such* a difference," Cackie said. "It lets in *so* much warmth in the winter months."

"Well I guess prob'ly!" Hattie said. "I always wanted to put in a window like that myself, bought a used one down to Eggle's in French Neck, stuck it out behind the barn. Before I could fix it, a storm cracked a branch off the old popple tree back there and smashed it to bits."

"What a shame," Fred said. "But we've found it doesn't pay to use old windows, you can't get them really tight."

"I guess that's true," Hattie said. She took a deep breath and said, "These the same old floors?" They used to be gouged and splintery, all the paint worn off. Now they were smooth and dark and glossy, with a prominent grain.

Cackie nodded. "We had Mr. Ransome sand and finish them. They came out quite well, don't you think?"

"Oh, *beautiful*," Hattie said.

She looked back at the kitchen, and her stomach contracted again. When the lightning killed Daddy she'd closed the door on his room and never let anyone use it for thirty years, and now— the sink was right where Daddy's bed had been! She looked away—and noticed the beams overhead. "Well by God would you look at that!" she said. "I seen them when I put up the celotex back in the fifties, but who ever thought they could turn out so nice?"

"Freddy's terribly clever," Cackie said. "Once we tore out that cardboard stuff—"

"The celotex?"

"Oh, is that what it's called? When we tore that out and exposed the beams, Fred instantly saw their potential. He hired some high school students to sand them down, then finished them with oil and turpentine."

"They look fine," Hattie said. "Real good." A huge refrigerator, new electric range, dishwasher... "Well," she said, "I gotta go."

"Oh you have to see the rest of the place," Cackie said. "It'll only take a minute."

"This way," Fred said, turning back toward the stairs, and Hattie followed.

More polished floors, another oriental rug, more beams, huge sliding glass doors to a deck. The paintings on the wall had frames with little lights on top, like the paintings in that art museum in Limerock Clara had dragged her into.

"What did you use this area for?" Fred asked with a quizzical smile.

"This was the old kitchen," Hattie said, "back when we had a dug well and hauled water with buckets. After we got the artesian well and piped the water in, it froze, 'cause there ain't no cellar under here. So we moved the kitchen to the other side, where it was when you bought the place, and turned this into the woodshed."

Cackie and Fred exchanged glances. "We insulated the crawlspace," Cackie said. "With urethane."

Hattie nodded. What was this woman trying to tell her—that she was a fool? She had banked with hay—and the pipe had split—but hay was free.

"We blew cellulose into the walls, even though we tore them down and put up plasterboard," Cackie said. "Fiberglass batts are too labor-intensive."

Hattie figured that meant they were too much work. Summer people were sort of allergic to work.

Her head was swimming. She could hardly remember the way things used to be. Oscar had died here, right where the summer people's piano was standing now. She'd wrapped his bad tooth in adhesive tape so the pliers wouldn't crack it up, but the damn thing shattered anyway, and what with him yelling and squirming around, she couldn't get all of it out. The pus went down into his lungs and my God he got hot, but Dr. Welsh said if they didn't pay up for Suzie's whooping cough he wouldn't come. The bedroom was freezing cold, so they'd moved Oscar into the kitchen, right next to the stove, but he'd died all the same.

"With the wall opened up, the view is superb," Cackie said. "So peaceful."

"Yeah," Hattie said, and her voice sounded distant and thin. She looked through the sliding glass doors at the spot that used to be her riding ring and a shock went through her. "My apple trees," she said.

Cackie tilted her head. "We hated to have to cut them down," she said, "but they blocked the view. Unfortunate."

"Yeah," Hattie said.

Those trees had been Jonathans, wonderful keepers, apples you couldn't buy in any store. For years they had been the only fruit they ate all winter, and now they were gone. She and Alfred had planted them back when Buddy was just a baby, and Cubby fell out of one once and broke his wrist. They must have been thirty years old. Good trees like that, cut down for a view.

Fred led the way through the door that used to go out back. Now it led to a hall, a bedroom with a gigantic closet and a downstairs bath. The shower was fiberglass, and the sink—dark blue—was set in a tan formica vanity. "Blue," Hattie said. It just slipped out, she hadn't meant it to.

"Isn't that color delightful?" Cackie said.

Hattie was frowning. "Well," she said, "I always liked a white bathroom myself."

At the head of the stairs was another, larger bath with another fiberglass tub and a *yellow* sink, and Hattie thought, How dirty *are* these people anyway? She always sponged down once a week and took a real bath once a month in the kitchen tub. Who needed more than that?

A washer and dryer sat against one wall, and the dryer was going—on a windy, sunny day like this! There was something wrong about that. She nodded at the washing machine. "Them automatics ain't all they're cracked up to be," she said. "I'll stick with my wringer. I like to be able to wash my clothes for as long as I want."

Cackie smiled her maddening smile and said, "But you can do that with an automatic, too, you simply reset the timer."

Hattie felt herself blush. "Oh, really?" she said. "I didn't know that."

The south bedroom had been transformed. She and all of her kids had been born in that room—all except Chuckie, that is, who had given her so much trouble. Hattie had always found if she stared at the dark brown stain where the chimney leaked, the pain didn't hurt so bad. Now the stain—the whole ceiling— was gone, and Hattie felt mad as hell, though she couldn't say why. After all, it was their house now.

In the north bedroom she said, "You sure got a lot of closets. I only had that tiny one downstairs."

"We're pretty thingy people," Fred said, grinning.

"Well, I guess," Hattie said.

She thought of when she was carrying Chuckie and had that growth on her neck. The bigger she got, the bigger the damn growth got. If she had it off, her baby would be retarded, Dr. Lord had said, but letting it go would kill her. So she had it off, of course—and Chuckie *was* retarded, just like Dr. Lord predicted, even though she'd had him at Lincoln General. Well, not *retarded,* he just couldn't read or count real good, but boy could he drive a car! She figured the growth was punishment for fooling around with Harlow, but then again Suzie wasn't Oscar's and turned out fine, got halfway through tenth grade. God must've been looking the other way that time—and a couple of other times, too.

Fred opened the door at the end of the hall. Hattie's heart felt thick.

The room looked twice as large as she remembered it, with a blue flowered print on the walls, two skylights, and wall-to-wall carpet, all white. "My God," she said.

"My study," Fred said.

"Why, who woulda guessed..." Her voice trailed off.

"Isn't it handsome?" Cackie said. "Fred loves the quiet here, and the light. What was it you used to call this room? You told us once."

"The open chamber," Hattie said.

Cackie nodded. "The open chamber. And what did you use it for?"

"Just storage," Hattie said—which was another lie. They'd kept the commode in here for when it got too cold and snowy to use the backhouse, and they'd hung the winter wash in here.

Through the window, the field shone and shook in the sun. In the bathroom, the dryer hummed.

As they went downstairs again, Cackie said, "It's certainly not a spacious house, but it's fine for just the two of us. Fixing the open chamber and building the new addition have helped a lot."

"I raised ten kids here," Hattie said.

"With your father's room closed off? And the open chamber used for storage? Amazing."

"We managed," Hattie said. At the foot of the steps she squinted at Cackie. "You people are gonna have kids, right? Didn't you tell me that?"

Cackie glanced at her husband, then smiled again. "We're not sure yet. Fred has his business, I have my photography..."

"Yeah," Hattie said.

When they'd come to her about buying the place, she had asked the same question and they'd told her, Yes, they were sure they would want to have children one of these days.

"And of course we have our cats," Cackie said.

"Of course," Hattie said, and thought: You call two animals having cats? She herself had sixteen cats, with more on the way.

They took her out back to show her the deck. The sheds where she'd kept her goats and pigs and tools had been torn down. And the blueberry field—had been plowed under! It was nothing but lawn! "The blueberries here, my God, we got quarts and quarts..."

Cackie said, "From those tiny little plants?"

"Best berries on the peninsula," Hattie said. A sudden knot hardened and burned in her ribs.

Around front Fred said, "*So* good to see you again. You'll have to come back when the landscaping's finished."

"Oh, yeah, I'll do that," Hattie said. "Thanks for showin' me through."

As she limped down the drive, the knot in her side made her catch her breath. She stopped, lit a Chesterfield, sucked it, exhaled. Smoke streamed away on the wind as she walked again.

Cubby was right, she thought, she should never have sold the place to these people, they'd wrecked everything she and Oscar and Alfred had done. They'd promised not to tear the place down, and they hadn't, but hadn't kept anything either: not the roof, the walls, the gardens, the sheds... And they'd lied about having kids. She coughed deeply, bringing up phlegm, which she spat at the field.

The pickup's door creaked loudly as she hauled herself inside. She sat there, smoking, staring at the house.

The pain had moved higher, close to her heart, and she thought, Oh these people are clever, all right, with their college degrees—cutting down apple trees it took thirty years to grow, plowing under the best blueberries in Maine, building a garage on the richest soil you'd ever want to find. Yeah, that's real clever.

What a fool she'd been. Cubby warned her, but she didn't listen. She'd sold the house for damn near nothing because these people said they would care for the land, have kids... Well, that was summer people for you, you couldn't trust them.

The copper flashing sparkled like a river full of coins. A blast of wind sent a shiver down Hattie's back.

The wind was like this in fifty-three, that time when Luke was playing with matches. They hadn't cut the field a second time that year because the tractor broke, and my God did it burn! They'd only had three brooms and it was beating them, but luck—for once—was on their side: the wind had changed, and the blaze took the chicken coop, sparing the house.

Hattie turned the ignition key and the pickup started. She revved the engine, thinking, Don't stall on me now. Don't you *dare* stall on me now. She looked at the house that was no longer hers, put the truck in gear, took a final drag on her cigarette, then flicked the butt into the field.

There was smoke for a minute, a sudden small flash, then the wind fanned a circle of copper into the hay.

Oh you're clever all right, Hattie thought as she pulled away. And you're probably lucky, too. Well, let's just see.

Uncle Cub at the Paradise Fair

Well now Cub was some pissed at LuAnn. He'd told her not to mess with him, and here she'd hauled him out of bed at noon. "Suzette says we gotta take Elton," was her excuse, but Cub thought the truth was she wanted to get his ass because Holcombe's had laid him off. He'd showed up late three times this week and they'd sent him out the door with fifty bucks and told him not to come back.

He drained his mug and slid it across the gold-flecked formica table. "You call that shit coffee?" he said. He was still in his undershorts.

LuAnn wiped the sink with her rag. "You think it ain't good enough, make it yourself," she said. She was putting on fat, especially around her ass.

A horn honked outside and Cub said, "Jesus Christ, that ain't Codfish already."

"Hell yes, who else?"

"He's too goddamn early."

"He ain't early, we gotta get Elton, go getcha pants on."

~

Codfish slouched behind the wheel, a cigarette loose in his fat white lips. The blue tattoo on his right arm screamed: EAT FISH! His car was a bashed-up Matador that just about cleared the ground. It was maybe the last one left in Maine, in the country, the whole damn world. One of its bumperstickers said GUN CONTROL MEANS USING BOTH HANDS. The other one said IF YOUR CAT IS MISSING LOOK UNDER MY WHEELS.

The back door let out a rusty groan as LuAnn yanked it wide.

The seat was shredded and covered with foam rubber crumbs. She batted some empty beer cans onto the floor.

Cub sat up front beside Codfish. They called him Codfish because he got hooked in the eye as a kid, and the plastic one gave him a fishy look. Also because of those fat white lips, and the codfishy whiskers, wiry and long, sticking out of his chin. He smelled like a goddamn codfish too. He worked down to Proteus Ocean Products, making compost out of guts, you could soak him in Aquafresh toothpaste a month and he'd still smell the same.

Cub picked up the half gallon bottle of coffee brandy that sat on the floor, unscrewed the top, and drank. "You ain't got milk?"

Codfish laughed in his foolish way, "Huk, huk," like a fishbone was caught in his throat. Some ashes fell over his T-shirt, which said ASS-KICKER FIRST CLASS. "I don't like it with milk," he said.

"Christ, that's how it's good," Cub said.

"Well we'll stop for some later."

"I want some now," Cub said, and scowled at the brandy. "We got any milk inside, LuAnn?"

"Nah, you used it all up in your coffee."

"We'll stop for some," Codfish said. He backed up fiercely, throwing up gravel and clouds of dust and making Howl, the doberman chained to the stake near the clothesline, bark like a son of a bitch.

"Old fuckin' Howl," Cub said. "If he was wearin' pants, he'd piss 'em."

The hole where the left rear window had been was covered with poly plastic and flapped with a vicious snapping sound as Codfish took off. Cub picked up the Camels that sat on the dash and lit up. The smoke made him cough way down deep in his chest. It sounded a lot like his mother's cough, like a bunch of wet marbles bouncing around down there.

Up the driveway they roared to Route One. On the other side of the road, on the top of Skunk Hill, Rollie Mink stared down hard from his cruiser. Rollie spent most of his life on Skunk Hill catching speeders and spying on Cub: you could see LuAnn's trailer and yard real good from up there. Rollie had taken Cub's license away three years ago, and was eager to catch him taking a turn at the wheel.

Three years ago Cub had been racing in Turtle's car, drove it home and was almost there, when Rollie Mink's cruiser shot out of the Skunk Hill lilacs and chased him into his dooryard, siren wailing. When Rollie came into the house Cub was really pissed off, and laid him straight out with a clamfork. That was it for his license. "A menace to society," the judge had called him. Cub got a charge out of that. You could still see the scar over Rollie's eyebrow, and always would.

As they passed him now, Cub gave him a twisting finger. "Goddamn it," LuAnn said, "you wanna get stopped? Codfish ain't got no sticker."

"Hell, Rollie can take a joke," Cub said, and drank from the brandy jug.

Codfish pulled up in front of Suzette's battered trailer and leaned on the horn. The three of them waited, smoking. The trailer's roof was covered with tires to keep it from blowing away. The screen was half gone from the door and the front wall was hammered up bad from last year's hail. Then Elton came out with a kick of the door, his hair sticking up in pale patches all over his head. He was ten now, but hadn't filled out at all. When Cub was ten he had lifted a hundred pound bag of cement, but Elton, Christ, the lawnmower pulled him all over the place. Well Suzette was skinny as a junkyard dog, it was probably on her side.

Elton went to the back of the car, but before he got in, Cub said, "Hey you got any milk in there?"

Elton stared. There was something a little wrong with the kid, one side of his face was flat. "Milk?" he said with a vacant look.

"Milk, Elton. The white stuff? From cows?"

Elton stood there a second then ran for the trailer, and soon he was back with a red quart container.

"Moo-Moo, my favorite brand," Cub said. "Okay, get in." Elton did, sitting next to LuAnn, and reamed out his nose with a finger.

Cub flipped the container open and swallowed some milk. "Hey Codfish, you know Elton, don't you, my halfass nephew?"

Codfish grinned, showing stumps of brown teeth, and lit out with a squeal.

Cub started to pour some milk in the brandy jug but Codfish said, "Don't put it in there, I don't want none in mine." Cub swigged some brandy, chased it with milk, and handed the carton to Elton, who said, "I'm hungry."

"Christ, you shoulda ate lunch," Cub said.

"I did."

"Well you'll wait'll the fair then. We'll get there in twenty minutes, that's all, you can hold out that long."

The sun was floating in yellow soup, LuAnn was sweating like a pig. "Pass that brandy back here," she said.

Cub did. "Ain't this weather some shitty," he said.

Codfish sucked on his cigarette. "Won't get no good weather till after the summer jerks leave," he said.

"Unless you can break it."

"An' how are you gonna do that?"

"Maybe paste some fat summer jerk's mouth," Cub said.

～

They got behind a pack of them out on the Paradise Road, New Yorkers cruising along in a shiny Lincoln, a tan one. Cub had been juicing all the way, he already had a good buzz on, and so when the Lincoln stopped at the four-way sign at Route Six he said, "Let's goose these fuckin' Jews!"

Codfish snuck up real slow, then whacked the Lincoln's bumper so hard that Elton fell back in his seat. Two of the Lincoln's passengers turned and its driver stared into his mirror, his eyes like a couple of golfballs. "That's it," Cub said, "take a good long look at a couple of genuwine Mainiacs, you jerks."

Codfish nudged them again. Elton giggled and said, "What's Jews?"

"New Yorkers," Cub said. "Summer jerks. They hate Jesus Christ an' they'll suck yer blood."

Elton's face was opaque.

"Uncle Cub's just kiddin'," LuAnn said.

The Lincoln made a sharp right turn that looked unplanned. "Bye-bye," Cub said, and flipped the stub of his cigarette out the window. "Be a hell of a good place to live if there wasn't no summer jerks here, right Elton?"

"I want a Slim Jim," Elton said.

Codfish snickered, "Huk, huk," and Cub said, "Christ, don't yer old lady feed ya?"

"Yeah," Elton said.

"Well she don't feed ya much, I guess, yer scrawny as a jailhouse rat."

"Can you get me a Slim Jim?"

"You see any place to get Slim Jims here? Maybe out in them trees?"

"What?"

"There's food at the fair," LuAnn said, looking pissed. "Five more minutes, okay?"

～

They parked in the field near the quarry. The car closed down hard with a death rattle cough. "Elton, gimme the milk," Cub said.

"It's gone," Elton said.

"What the hell do you mean it's gone?"

"I drunk it."

"What?!"

Elton's smile was sick. "I was thirsty," he said.

LuAnn kicked her door open. "Jesus, we'll get more milk inside," she said.

They got out. The cars all around them had summer jerk plates. Codfish leaned on his bumper to tie his shoe and the bumper fell onto the ground. "Huk, huk, hit that Lincoln a little too hard," he said. "Well, leave it lay."

They walked toward the tents, Codfish bouncing along, his Camel real loose in his lips. He was high on the brandy and tripped on a little stone. The ashes flew from his cigarette, he looked surprised, then laughed.

"There's a ferris wheel!" Elton cried.

"Ain't you the perceptive one," Cub said.

"What's that mean?" Elton said.

"It means yer smart."

"Oh."

"Don't lie to the kid," LuAnn said. "You want him to grow up confused?"

Cub paid for them all. If the kid hadn't been there he would of snuck in, but he didn't want Elton to think he was crooked. Anyway, he had fifty bucks severance pay—fifty *tax-free* bucks, cash money, and none of the goddamn welfare bums would get a nickel of it.

People were throwing baseballs at shit, tossing pennies at shit, there was rock 'n roll racket and tootley carnival music. Out on the track, cars were racing around. Elton stared at it all and said, "I'm hungry."

The brandy jug tight in his fist, Cub went to the nearest refreshment booth. "Gimme a Slim Jim," he said.

"And a whoopie pie," Elton said.

"Yeah, a goddamn whoopie pie too, an' a couple of pints of milk."

"Ain't got no milk." The guy was fat, with short gray hair and spiderweb veins on his nose and cheeks.

Cub paid. "Well where can I get some?"

The fat man shrugged. "In town, I guess."

Elton chomped on the Slim Jim, kicking up dust. Cub went up to LuAnn. "You told me we'd get some milk in here," he said. "Well where?"

"They gotta have it *somewhere*," LuAnn said.

But they didn't. Cub tried five booths. "Goddamn you, LuAnn," he said. "Can I have another whoopie pie?" Elton asked. His mouth was all brown from the first one, and Codfish laughed. They drank from the bottle. "I want some goddamn *milk!*" Cub said. He needed it now, the brandy was burning his gut.

The stock car race was winding down. Codfish hung on the chain-link fence. Cars skidded and screeched, whooshed, twisted, spun into each other. Elton gobbled his second whoopie pie, eyes wide, and asked, "Uncle Cub, can you drive like that?"

"Shit yes," Cub said. "Used to drive like that all the time."

"Ain't *that* the truth," said LuAnn with a smirk. "And now he can't drive at *all.*"

"Just shut yer trap," Cub said. LuAnn was getting more like Suzette every day.

Whoopie pie cream was up Elton's nose. "Did you *really?*" he said.

"Wipe that shit off yer face," Cub said.

The race was over. The loudspeaker said that the next one would be in an hour. People drifted away. "Why don't you take Elton up on a ride?" LuAnn said.

Cub was gazing away at the stalls where the animals were, and ignored the question. "Gimme yer goddamn soda cup," he said. With a scowl LuAnn swallowed the rest of her Moxie and handed it over.

Cub walked past the rabbits and goats and went up to the cows. A Holstein was lying there lazily chewing. A fat blue ribbon was tacked to the front of its stall. "Shit yes, the real thing," Cub said, and he opened the gate.

"Come on, get up!" he said to the Holstein, and whacked her rump hard with the flat of his hand. She glared, offended, but didn't budge. People stopped and stared. Cub reared back and booted the cow and she staggered up, moaning. A little girl said, "What's that man doing, Mommy?"

Cub yanked on the Holstein's udder and milk dribbled over his hand. The plastic cup was halfway full when a woman's voice shouted, "You! Stop that! Get away from my cow!"

She looked like a summer jerk in her round white hat. "Christ, lady," Cub said, "what's yer problem? I'm milkin' the goddamn thing, not fuckin' it."

The woman turned red and began to scream. "Get out! Get out or I'll call the police!" A crowd ringed the stall. Cub looked at his cup. Half a pint. It would have to do. He farted as loud as he could and walked away.

LuAnn was up on the Whirl-A-Way with Elton. "Pie eating contest in fifteen minutes!" the loudspeaker said. Cub went looking for Codfish. He found him down by the grandstand watching a horse pull a shitload of granite blocks. Codfish crushed out his Camel and said, "You got yer milk."

"Damn right," Cub said.

Codfish swigged from the bottle, then Cub poured a wallop of brandy into the warm, rich milk. He drank. "This makes that store shit taste like chalk," he said.

They watched the horse. It strained at the load, barely able to budge it. Its owner kept flicking its flank with a whip, yelling "Hi!" and the sucker kept pulling—then suddenly stopped, dropped down on its knees and puked blood, spasmed, rolled on its side and lay still. A man with a pipe and a plaid sports jacket muttered, "Barbaric."

Cub wanted to paste him one. "You see what ya get for workin' too hard?" he said, and Codfish said, "Damn right," and lit up a Camel.

Cub frowned at the prostrate horse. "That's it," he said. "That's it right there."

Elton came up with LuAnn and said, "How's come the horse fell down?"

"Worked too hard and it killed him," Cub said drinking out of his cup.

Elton stared at the corpse. "I'm hungry," he said.

"For Christ's sake, Elton—"

The loudspeaker broke in, announcing the start of the pie eating contest. Cub snagged Elton's arm. "Okay," he said, "we'll fill you up right now."

He jerked Elton over the path to the contest table. A shitload of kids were sitting there, hands tied behind them, a large-size blueberry pie waiting under each chin.

"Here's another bozo for you," Cub told the guy in charge. His back was all twisted, like someone had tried to screw him right into the ground. The guy had Elton sit on a bench while he tied his hands. Elton stared at the pie in front of him and said, "I don't like this kind."

"Well that's the only kind they got," Cub said. "This is blueberry day at the fair, Elton, that's all they got."

A couple more latecomers sat and were bound. Then the twisted guy went to the head of the table and said, "Okay, you all ready?" One blond-headed girl just kept running her mouth. "Begin!"

Heads plunged into the pies. Elton sat there. "Start eatin'," Cub said. "You said you was hungry, now eat."

"I don't like blueberry—"

"Eat it!" Cub shouted, and shoved Elton's face at the pie. He went in it up to the eyeballs and came out gasping. The twisted guy said, "No helping or he'll be disqualified."

"I don't give a shit about that," Cub said, "I just wanna fill his gut. Now eat!"

Elton did, his face totally blue. Other kids dived at their pies with abandon, snorting and drooling. They backed out coughing, blue hunks falling out of their mouths, then plowed in again.

"You full yet, Elton?"

Yes, Elton nodded. His mouth was choked.

"No you ain't! Now eat!"

Elton sank into filling and crust. Blue lumps on his cheeks made him look like he had a disease.

"Time's up!" the twisted man proclaimed.

Elton wearily spat out some pie and it plopped in his lap. His mouth hung slack. He was blue as a week-old corpse as he turned his eyes up to Cub. "Did I win?" he asked.

"Did you win. How the hell could you win, you left half your pie. That kid down the end ate the whole damn thing."

"Well he's fatter than me," Elton said.

"That ain't no excuse. Some of the biggest eaters I ever seen was skinny, just look at Codfish. You still hungry?"

"No."

"Well good."

"I'm just thirsty."

Cub narrowed his eyes. He felt like squeezing the kid's crooked head straight, he musta got caught in the wringers when he was born, what a friggin' dip.

Codfish came up with LuAnn. "Can you buy me a Moxie?" Elton asked.

"Go get hosed off first," LuAnn said glaring at Cub.

Elton stood in the hose line and got washed down, then they went to a food booth and got him a Moxie. The Pirate Ship was rocking hard, the ferris wheel was whipping around, and the dude at the hootchie-kootchie tent was starting to make his pitch.

"I wanna go see the exhibits," LuAnn said. "The quilts an' all."

Cub poured the last of the brandy into his cup. No more milk, so he said, "Gimme some of that Moxie, Elton."

Elton gave up his drink with a sour face. Cub sloshed out some ice cubes and half of the Moxie, tasted the mixture and said, "That ain't half bad."

Elton snatched up his cup and drank. Then his eyes went wide, his cup hit the ground, and he clapped both hands to his throat.

"Cough it up!" cried LuAnn, but Elton kept choking.

Cub shoved his cup at the startled Codfish, then ran behind Elton and hugged him hard under the ribs. Elton wheezed like a tire losing air but his face kept turning red, so Cub stuck a quick middle finger down his throat. Up came the ice cube, followed by blueberry pie.

Elton gasped, his chest heaving, blue drool spinning down from his chin.

"Take him with you," Cub said, shaking pie off his hand. Codfish gave him his brandy. He finished it off.

"Well where you goin'?" LuAnn asked.

"Exhibits," Cub said.

LuAnn narrowed her eyes. "Yeah? What kinda exhibits?"

"Just take him!" Cub said. He was feeling some mean now, the sides of his head were all clogged. And this heat! He walked off with Codfish, who snickered and smoked.

The hootchie-kootchie tent was blazing hot. It smelled like horseshit, hay, and sweat, and the sunlight that oozed through its canvas made everything yellow. The crowd was all men, they were packed in tight, and Cub pushed his way toward the front, Codfish right on his heels. Eddie Walters was there, and Harold Milt, looking deathbed sick in the yellow light. Codfish snickered, "Huk, huk."

"What the hell are you laughin' at?" Cub said.

"There's Perley Figg."

Cub craned his neck and sure enough, there was Perley right next to the stage. "What a horney old fart," Cub said. "Christ, he's seventy-six."

"You still gonna make it at seventy-six?"

"Hell no, I'll be dead, like that horse."

Sudden whistles and cheers as the music started and the girl traipsed out. She had three rolls of fat at her waist and a tooth was gone, but she settled right down to business and took off her top. She pivoted, showing her chink-yellow ass and its blue and red snake tattoo. Her cheeks sagged worse than the old lady's barn, but everyone hollered and clapped. A tug at her G-string and off it came, and Codfish laughed, "Huk, huk."

Cub got hit with an elbow and somebody tread on his foot. The noise and the heat were making him wicked ugly. The girl faced front and the boys went ape. Perley Figg raised his fist in the air.

"Come on," Cub said, and pushed his way forward.

"Where to?" Codfish said.

"Just come on!"

Some of the boys didn't like being shoved, but Cub cut them off with a sneer. He came up behind Perley Figg, looked at Codfish and said, "You ready?"

The two of them grabbed Perley's elbows and lifted him up. His toothless old mouth went wide and he squeaked, "Lemme down!"

The girl stopped dancing. Snarls and boos from the crowd.

Cub and Codfish shoved Perley right onto the stage. He landed beside the girl, who started to scream. A bald guy ran out from the wings and hollered, "Hey!"

"Old Perley just got a new pacemaker, number six," Cub said. "He can take the excitement."

"What?" The bald guy was red as a lobster. "You can't interrupt the show!"

"Well it looks like we done it," Cub said.

The girl was just standing there, naked and shaking, and Perley stood up and broke into a grin. Guys cheered. Cub noticed a mean wicked scar on the the girl's sagging gut as a voice near his elbow said, "How's come Codfish and you threw that man up there?"

"Elton! Jesus, I told you to stick with LuAnn!"

"I didn't like them quilts."

"Well you ain't allowed in here!"

The bald guy was totally wild now. "I'll have you arrested! You can't—"

"See this kid here?" Cub said, clutching Elton's pale neck. "He's ten years old, I'll have *you* arrested!" The bald guy looked thunderstruck. Perley Figg was still grinning; it pissed Cub off.

Pulling Elton behind him, he got the hell out of the place.

"How's come the lady took off all her clothes?" Elton said as LuAnn came up. "Because it was hot in there," Cub said. "Christ almighty, LuAnn, I thought you was watchin' this turkey."

"He checked out on me, I searched everywhere."

"Not everywhere, I found him in the goddamn hootchie-kootchie tent."

"An' that ain't all you found, I bet."

Cub felt like booting her fat white ass. Elton said, "Look! They're startin' the races again!"

They walked to the fence. Some hotshots were roaring their motors and checking out this and that. Cub's head was as big as a basketball, dark as night.

Then he noticed the Charger. He'd had one up on blocks for six years now; it was rusted solid. This one here was a beauty, blue and gold, that sparkly kind of blue like diamond dust. Number 50 to top it all off, his lucky number. The car of his dreams, and his heart shifted gears.

"I'm hungry again," Elton said.

The night that was swelling Cub's head became brilliant day as he ran through the gate. The motor was already running. He jumped in the driver's seat and roared away. In the rearview mirror some idiots waved their arms. He laughed like mad.

The first car he'd driven in almost a year, and Jesus did it feel good! Shit, this sucker could *move!* Good and noisy, too! Dust rose in a spiraling cyclone cloud as the needle hit seventy-five.

The second turn around the track he heard the siren, and there was the goddamn cop. Okay, he'd beat the son of a bitch, and he jammed his foot to the floor. Ninety-eight, ninety-nine... The world was a blur, smears of yellow and silver and blue...

The roadblock came up too fast. He slammed on the brakes and went into a spin, whipped around three times, smacked a cruiser, bounced into the fence. He'd hit his head on something, his hair was wet. The crowd hung onto the ruptured fence and stared.

"Let's see your license," the cop said and shit, it was Rollie Mink.

Cub glared at the clamfork scar above Rollie's eye. "Shit, you know I ain't got no license, Rollie."

"You're under arrest."

"Well screw you, too."

"You're a goddamn menace to society, goddamn it!"

"You bet yer ass."

"And you give me the finger back there on Skunk Hill."

"Damn right. And here's one for good luck."

As they took him away in the cruiser he heard Elton say: "Uncle Cub! You drove good!"

~

Codfish came in the morning. LuAnn was getting the bail together, he said. "Oh yeah, somethin' else, yer old man died."

"You mean Buster?" Cub said.

"Yeah, Buster."

"He ain't my old man, he just brung me up, Perley Figg's my old man."

"No shit."

"Hell yes. Still a horney old sucker at seventy-six."

Codfish laughed, "Huk, huk."

Cub frowned. "Well maybe I oughta tell Elton," he said.

"Yeah?"

"That I'm his old man, I mean."

"Maybe so."

"What a dip," Cub said, and he closed one eye half way. "That was good yesterday, that Charger was great. But now LuAnn's pissed, I bet."

"Not too pissed."

"She'll need plenty of lovin'."

"Well I guess prob'ly!" Codfish said. He took out his Camels and shook one loose. "Rained last night. Clear today. Cool, too."

"I broke the goddamn weather some good," Cub said.

The Best in the World

After the funeral, out on the deck his father had built and Danny had never seen before, his mother said, "I don't know what I'll do."

He looked away from her hollow eyes and across the water—at distant islands black in the April sun—then looked at the tiers of wire lobster traps beside the barn. Uncle Mike, his fingers stained with thirty years of grease and motor oil, was filling his plate with triangular thin white sandwiches, lobster and seafood salad. Danny had not touched the food.

In a weary voice, his mother said, "Mike knows a fella down to Weeks who wants to buy it all. I could sure use the money, but I don't know. Sometimes I think I should give it to Eddie Marsh, he helped your father so much. I can't understand why he didn't show up at the funeral."

Danny looked at the water again. A breeze brought a quick touch of winter cold. They'd been lucky to hit an April day in the sixties so people could be outdoors.

Uncle Mike ate a tiny sandwich in two huge bites. Danny looked at his mother again. She had gotten so old so fast. The past two years had been terribly hard. And *I wasn't here to help,* he thought.

"To sell that boat..." his mother said.

Tears were rising again, and Danny held her. "Don't sell anything just yet," he said. "Let me talk to Toby."

~

On the plane, the clouds below him looked like a white, plowed field. He thought of the traps against the barn, he thought of his mother's worried face, he thought of what Toby had said last week.

Toby had just missed out on the part in *False Impressions,* and this time *he* was the one who talked about moving.

"Moving where?" Danny said.

"Anyplace but here!" Toby said as he poured more gin in his glass. He was already drunk.

"You'll consider Maine?"

Rolling his soft blue eyes, Toby said, "Oh, I suppose. "But it's always so *cold.* On top of that, nobody's *there.*"

"You'll get used to the cold," Danny said.

"Sure. Southern California Man Found Frozen Stiff."

"It's not that bad. And the people in Maine are real, Tobe— real solid folks with their feet on the ground."

"I think that's what scares me," Toby said. "They probably celebrate Veterans' Day and things like that." He swallowed more gin. "God knows it's beautiful there, and quiet, and clean, but for *us*... I mean what will they think if you move back there with—?"

"An outtastater?"

"Right," Toby said with a laugh.

"Things are different there now," Danny said. "Most people are willing to live and let live."

"Really."

"Really. I think we should do it. What's left for us here? We've been trying for almost twelve years to break through, and we're still waiting tables."

"I know, I know," Toby said with his hand in his thinning, tinted hair. "But *Maine.*" He looked at the floor, at the Persian rug. "Maybe this thing with Petrellis will help me decide."

"Maybe so."

Toby frowned. "People really don't lock their doors in Maine?"

"They really don't."

"It's hard to believe."

"You'd like it—in spite of the cold," Danny said.

Three days later his mother called to tell him his father had died, and the day after that he was headed to Maine.

And now here he was in L.A again. The plane landed softly; some people clapped.

In the terminal Toby was there and his eyes were wet as he said, "Petrellis wouldn't even *audition* me, he told me I look too old."

≈

The first place Ted Harris wanted to show them was Eddie Marsh's old house. Some outtastaters had fixed it up about ten years ago. Danny said that he wasn't interested. They looked at a half dozen other places, and settled on one at the end of a gravel lane. A family named Harper had lived there when Danny was growing up.

"I can *breathe*," Toby said leaning back in his leather recliner and spreading his arms. The chair looked totally out of place in the old farmhouse. "My postnasal drip is *gone,* for the first time *ever.* And so far I have to agree with you, people in Maine are really nice. They're so *friendly,* so *helpful.*"

"They're great," Danny said, "the best in the world." He looked through the window at pines and hackmatacks, and thought of Eddie Marsh.

≈

Eddie's father had worked in the woods, and his mother— before the injury to her back—had packed fish at Paradise Packing. His sisters had worked at Paradise too until they got pregnant—and pregnant and pregnant. His brothers—seven of them? Eight?—had clammed and hunted and torn apart rundown cars. Even in winter, most of the living went on outdoors, and the house was a shambles, smelly and dark, with holes in the plaster walls. One time Danny had entered the kitchen and found a hunting knife stuck in the floor and a chicken perched on top of the battered fridge.

Danny had grown up with Eddie Marsh. Eddie had been the only boy his age within half a mile, and all through grade school Danny had roamed the woods and coves with him, caught smelts and mackerel with him, swum in Treacher's Pond with him on sultry summer days. It was Eddie who taught him how to shoot: a twenty-two first, then a thirty-ought six.

Eddie, in turn, had learned about lobster fishing from Danny, and took to it right from the start. The summer when Danny turned twelve and bought his own outboard, Eddie had worked with him practically every day. Coming back in with a flock of gulls crying above them one bright afternoon, Eddie said: "We should go into business together, buy us a lobster boat together," and Danny surprised himself by saying, "No, I'm not staying in Maine."

Eddie frowned. "What?"

"I want to see other places," Danny said. "And I don't want to be a lobsterman all my life."

"Well why the hell not? It's good money."

"I don't want to get up at four in the morning and bait and haul traps every day," Danny said. "I want to do something clean, where it's sunny and warm." He knew that was only part of it. There was more—lots more—that he didn't yet understand.

"And your mother and father, what about them?" Eddie said. "When they're old, you ain't gonna be here to help them?"

"Maybe I'll come back then," Danny said. "But before that, I just have to live my own way."

Looking back on it now, it seemed that Eddie had known what that way would be before Danny himself had known. The last time they'd gone for a swim in Treacher's Pond—at the age of fifteen—they were sunning themselves on the rocks when Eddie had sat up quickly, blinking sharply, as if he had felt Danny's eyes on his muscular body. He'd frowned and put his clothes back on, and was silent as they rode their bikes back home.

That November, Danny shot his one and only deer. He had seen Eddie less and less as the year wore on, but there had been promises made about hunting, and Eddie kept his promises. When Danny hit his doe, it stumbled, blood soaking its front, and crashed through a stand of puckerbrush before its legs collapsed. Eddie told him to shoot it again, but he couldn't, so Eddie did, once, in the head, and Danny threw up. "Okay, let's dress it," Eddie said, and Danny said, "No, I can't," and walked away, and Eddie spat on the leaf-matted earth and cursed and did it himself. And things had never been right between them again.

Eddie dropped out of school the next year, at the age of sixteen—by the time Danny knew the truth.

He had known since the prom. When he wouldn't kiss Alice Carter in front of her house, she said, "Danny, some people say— I mean—" He closed his eyes, dizzy and faint as she said, "But I don't believe them. Come into the house with me, nobody's home, and I'll prove it's not true, I'll prove it." And that was his first and last time with a woman, and proved everything he had feared, and Alice had cried.

He saw Eddie once after that, late that summer. Danny was leaving the funeral parlor when Eddie came out of his pickup and walked up the speckled gray granite steps. When he saw Danny coming he lowered his head, but Danny stopped him— caught his wrist—and said, "I'm sorry."

Eddie jerked his arm away; his mouth was mean. "You're goin' away, ain'tcha, Danny?" he said. "*Your* mother's still livin' and you're gonna *leave* her." His teeth were rotted, he smelled of beer. Staggering backward he said, "Too good for us, ain'tcha? Too good for your mom and dad, ain'tcha? Only friggin' kid they got, and you're runnin' off." He spat on the granite and said, "Well then get the hell out and don't come back, we don't need faggots here."

The words had stung like salt in a wound. And whenever Eddie came to mind in L.A., that night outside the funeral home was part of the memory.

His sophomore year at USC, Danny went to a party, drank too much, and woke up the following morning in bed with a man, his memories blurred but pleasant. The man was a fellow acting student, thin and blond, with bitter wit and a high-pitched, biting laugh. The relationship lasted for nearly six months, and when it was over, Danny no longer had doubts about what he was.

He met Toby in graduate school. After the third time they slept with each other, they moved in together. Twelve years ago now. In all those years they had done some commercials for hair dye and managed to get a few minor parts in some short-lived sitcoms, and that was it. Then Toby had fallen ill last winter—seriously ill. Intestinal obstruction, surgery, and one night Danny had come home to find him in tears.

"I'm so *tired*," he said. "I'm so tired of trying to *make* it, it's so *degrading*. I've got to stop. If I don't, I'll get really ill."

Danny sat down beside him. "You're right," he said. "I'm ready to pack it in too. Who needs this stuff?   Let's just be normal people for once in our lives."

Toby sniffed. "*Normal* people."

"You know what I mean," Danny said. "Real jobs, security, stability. We're thirty-four. We'll die if we keep this up."

But Toby had felt much better the following week and changed his mind: he would give it another shot after all. He auditioned three times and was turned down twice, then waited and waited to hear about *False Impressions*, a big budget movie. When they told him he hadn't made it, he drank until he was sick. He was waiting to hear from Mark Petrellis, casting director of *All My Loves,* when Danny's mother called with the terrible news.

~

Danny sat at the table across from her now, the same kitchen table they'd had when he was a kid. It was maple, rectangular, draped with a checkered red tablecloth, and stood in front of the window that faced the bay.

His mother looked into her mug, then sipped her coffee. The joints of her fingers were knobby and stiff. "Eddie Marsh did so much for your father these past two years," she said. "Helped fix his traps, helped haul..."

"Did he ever talk about me?"

"No, never. Whatever went wrong between you two?"

"We just drifted apart." Danny looked at his mug. "Where's he live?"

"Curtis Point, where the Bradfords were."

"Is he married?"

"Divorced. His wife has the kids."

Danny turned to the window. "Still using the same color buoys, I see."

"Same color. I hear he has eight hundred traps."

"God, eight hundred blaze orange buoys out on that bay."

His mother smiled—one of the very rare smiles he'd seen these past few days. "He'd have four hundred more if you hadn't come back."

"I'm glad I did."

His mother kept smiling. "It's going to be wonderful seeing you out on the water again."

"It's going to feel wonderful too," Danny said. "It's good to be home."

"I'm glad you feel that way," his mother said. She looked at her mug. "How's Toby doing?"

"Fine," Danny said. "He's a true city boy, but he's really enjoying himself."

"That's good."

Danny wanted to keep on going, to talk about it, but couldn't. He'd never been able to talk about it. So? She knew the truth. He looked at her, her smile died, the space between them seemed to cool. He drank the last of his coffee and rinsed out his cup.

The first of the fifty wire traps slid over the rail and was gone in a flash. Danny had fished wooden traps as a kid, had loved to watch them darken and disappear in the depths of the bay. There was something hypnotic about how they sank, something almost mystical in it. Danny had never dared talk about that with his father. "A man who's got time to watch traps go down sure ain't gonna make much money," he would've said—that or its equivalent.

Fifty today and fifty tomorrow and fifty for six days after that. The gear was in excellent shape—thanks to Eddie Marsh.

The red and blue buoys bobbed in the sun, the string of them stretching back toward land, into Danny's past. This was the first time he'd lobstered in sixteen years, and it felt like he'd never been gone. Packing the bait bags, shoving them into the trap with the iron...everything felt right. He'd never realized how deep fishing ran in his blood. Seeing these colors bright on the water again made him feel that a part of his father still lived. He knew that his mother would feel the same thing.

Another trap over and gone to the sea. The frantic hopes of Hollywood were fading fast against the tough reality of Maine. Toby had landed a job with Porter Real Estate, and so far he liked it. Things were going to be just fine—till winter, anyway.

Everywhere he went he saw blaze orange, and just before ten o'clock a boat appeared, a man gaffed one of those orange buoys, then hauled the trap up on his block. He was bearded and wearing a Red Sox cap and yellow oil gear. He hurriedly threw back crabs and shorts, rebaited and tossed the trap over again. Danny yelled, "Eddie! Hey!" but the boat made a wild, throbbing turn and took off.

~

When Danny walked through the door that afternoon, Toby was waiting, drink in hand, face flushed, his smile bright. "I sold a house!" he said. "Third day on the job, and I actually sold a house! I'm a *success!*"

"Fantastic," Danny said, and Toby laughed. "Good grief, just look at you! The grizzled old salt, right out of a forties movie! Ayuh, some good haulin' today, huh, matey?" He wrinkled his nose. "Boy, are you ever *pungent.*"

"You're in it all day, you don't even smell it," Danny said.

Fanning his face with his hand, Toby said, "Well *I* sure do."

"From now on, I'll take my stuff off in the entryway. So you sold a *house.*"

Toby grinned. "An *expensive* one, too, on the water." He

drank. "I hate to tell you this, but it sold to an outtastater, a Masshole."

"Who else has the money to buy on the water?"

"Sad," Toby said, "but true." He drank. "I *love* this job," he said. "I'm *good* at this."

"I knew you would be," Danny said. He shook his head. "Man, I am beat."

"Surprise, surprise," Toby said. "Up to your elbows in rotten fish at four o'clock in the morning, loading the traps on your boat then tossing them into the water hither and yon. Talk about a long *day*."

"I'm out of shape."

"You need a drink."

"First I need to get cleaned up."

"I won't disagree with you *there*."

When Danny came down from his shower, Toby walked up and kissed his cheek, then gave him his martini. "A toast," he said. "To us, to our new life."

They clinked their glasses together, drank, and Toby said, "To home sweet home. It really is starting to *feel* like home, I see what you *mean* about this place. I can breathe, I'm relaxed, and Liz Porter is just so pleasant to work for, she's so *polite*. She makes the people in Hollywood look like three year olds. You act civil out there and they think you're *weak*."

"We've made the right decision," Danny said.

"I know it. Just one question. When do the leaves come out? I mean, it's *May*."

"Soon," Danny said. "At about the time the werewolves start to roam."

"Oh, funny, funny," Toby said, rolling his big blue eyes.

◠

Danny was out at dawn again with fifty more traps, the air sharp and cool in his lungs. He thought of L.A., its burning smog, and laughed. The icy dark days were months away—the days when Toby would learn the truth about Maine—and a summer of long bright northern evenings stretched ahead of them.

As he passed Crow Island he saw a buoy, one of *his* buoys, red and blue, right up by the shore, near the rocks. His heart sank.

Up ahead was another one, not where he'd set out a trap. He idled over and gaffed it and up it came.

His father's proud colors, cut. The line had been cut and the trap was gone. He tossed the buoy onto the floor of the boat and knew that wherever he went he would find the same thing—every one of his lines would be cut.

He thought of that night long ago on the steps of the funeral home, heard Eddie's hot bitter words. Around him danced buoys of different designs: blue and green, red and black, blue with only a thin stripe of white—and blaze orange.

He revved his engine, turned around and headed back to shore. The mainland flared up in the gold of the rising sun like a healing dream: dark spruce, a clear blue sky, the clean white faces of sturdy houses—the hard cold beauty he'd walked away from sixteen years ago.

In his mind he could see Eddie Marsh turn his boat away sharply, could see Toby raising his glass. *To home sweet home,* he could hear Toby saying.

Another buoy, dead ahead, was cut and floating free. As he went to retrieve it, Danny thought, *Yeah, Toby, home sweet home.*

Detour

Steve had a hard time finding the place. The directions Anne had given him said you went down Route One to the Brisbane Road, turned left, took the tarred road after the gravel pit, turned right on the first dirt road. But somehow he missed the Brisbane Road and had to go back, and then when he took the tarred road after the gravel pit and went two miles without finding any dirt road, he turned around, drove back to the Brisbane Road, tried the next tarred road, found no roads at all off that for over a mile. He went to the first tarred road again, and this time, three miles down, he found it: Stickney Lane. It was just about wide enough for two cars and in very poor shape, with dense broad weeds growing up on both sides.

He drove down it slowly, skirting the major potholes, passing a field on his right and a gaunt dead towering elm that had lost all its bark, and suddenly there was the house. He pulled to the side of the road and stopped and sat there staring at the place.

An ancient cape, its ridge pole swaybacked, cedar shingles silvered and curled, the paint all but gone from its trim; only a few dull aqua chips still clung to its sills and window frames. On its door, once white but yellowed by time and sun, hung a Christmas wreath, although it was early May.

Beside the house was a shed, its doors made of unplaned boards. It too was covered with weathered shingles, and stacked against its broad south wall was a modest pile of wire lobster traps. A large old battered hoodless car sat up to its windows in weeds at the edge of a field. Steve adjusted his glasses for a better look. A Cadillac, about twenty years old, its headlights gone, its blue paint chalky and dull. Off to its right was a tilting outhouse, also made of unplaned boards, partly hidden in a stand of sumac.

The cape was about thirty feet from the road. A big brown sedan with rusted fenders sagged in the dooryard, and rather than park behind it, Steve stayed on Stickney Lane. A dog was chained to a stake in the dirt front yard, and as Steve cut the engine, the animal jumped up and started to bark in an ugly way. Steve picked up his briefcase, opened his door and got out.

The day was cool, with a low gray sky. It had rained in the night, and a giant puddle lay to the left of the path leading up to the door. A mailbox was perched on a tilted post at Steve's end of the rutted path. It was dented and rusty, the crooked number 423 in white on its dark green side. Its flag was missing and so was its door. As Steve approached it, the dog rushed forward, its yellow teeth bared, and was yanked back hard by its chain, which kept it just short of the path. It growled and snarled, its lips curled up, as Steve walked by. Its fur was streaks of yellow and black and its eyes were a silvery blue. Steve guessed it was husky and chow. He knocked on the door. The large pane of glass above the wreath made a buzzing sound.

He waited, his eyes on the wreath. Its needles had turned the color of rust and its red velvet bow, now pink in spots, was limp and dirty and torn. He looked to his right, at the picture window, and thought he saw something move. The dog kept barking. Steve waited.

To the left of the house, maybe twenty feet off, an amputated apple tree was showing signs of coming back from winter's long brutality. The lowest of its three remaining limbs held a rope and a threadbare tire. Steve knocked again, sparking the dog into fresh fits of rage. The torn thin curtain behind the glass shivered slightly then, and the door came open a crack.

The woman had spikes of bright red-orange hair that

sprouted like weeds from her patchy scalp. Her wide white face was heavily lined. She squinted hard. Her eyes were the same silver blue as the dog's.

"Mrs. Taggart?"

She nodded.

"Steve Hillman. I called a while ago?"

The woman kept squinting, as if she had trouble hearing.

"I'm sorry I'm late, I got lost."

The woman kept squinting.

"Anne Collins gave me your name," Steve said. "The public health nurse?"

The woman's right eyelid twitched and she licked her lips. "Oh yeah, Anne Collins," she said, looking down. She stood there motionless, looking—at what? His shoes? The threshold?—then finally she opened the door.

Steve stepped into the kitchen. A powerful acrid tang burned the back of his nose: cat excrement, urine. He looked at the white steel sink, a huge stack of dishes drowning in greasy gray water, and then at the table, the little girl sitting there. She was skinny and pale and blond and dirty and strikingly beautiful. He looked past the splintered and scarred door jamb to the room off the kitchen. A packing crate standing on end, at least six feet tall, spewed dozens of broken and dirt-caked dolls across a green scalloped rug. On top of the crate was a small black and white TV with half an antenna. A fuzzy soap opera was on.

The kitchen table stood under the picture window. The child sat on its far side, in front of the green gas range. Steve went to the chair directly across from the window. The floor was sticky under his feet. "Okay if I sit here?" he asked.

"Oh sure," Mrs. Taggart said. She frowned and blinked, then lowered herself with deliberate slowness into the chair on Steve's right, the one nearest the door.

Steve sat in the spoke-backed wooden chair. Its cream-colored shiny enamel was peeling away, revealing a dark dull green. It tilted slightly to the left and its seat felt damp on his thighs. He set his briefcase down on the sticky linoleum rug and took out a yellow lined tablet. The rug, brick-red, was cracked and cupped and scattered with clumps of fur.

The child glanced at him furtively, instantly looking down as he caught her eye. She was wearing a dirty torn T-shirt and shorts and was barefoot. Her skin was so pale it was almost translucent, her nostrils were rimmed with black, and her blond hair was tangled and dull. Her eyes were grayer than her mother's, but had that same silvery tint. She held a clump of brown Play-Doh in her grimy fist, and squashed it onto the table, rolling it, shoving it into a cluster of chicken bones.

"Anne told me you're having a lot of financial problems," Steve said quietly, taking a pen from his jacket pocket.

Mrs. Taggart's mouth came open, as if she were going to speak, then suddenly snapped shut. She blinked, and a giant tear rolled down her cheek and landed on her soiled blue work shirt, making a nickle-sized blotch just above her right breast. "Vernon left me," she said in a wavering, mournful voice. "He come back and took all his tools, and once they do that, they mean it. He's gone."

"You don't work," Steve said, his eyes on the stain on her shirt.

"Oh no, no, no," Mrs. Taggart said. She shook her head with a rhythmic slowness, as if in time to a tune. "Can't work, hurt my leg, cut it right to the bone with my chainsaw six years ago. Ain't never been right since then. Them doctors, they say...they're supposed to be good...oh, I don't know..." She frowned at the plastic tablecloth. Its checks were various shades of blue, about two inches square.

"You have no source of income?"

"No." It was almost a whisper.

"How many children do you have?"

Mrs. Taggart breathed deeply, audibly, then exhaled. Her breasts were broad and flat and low beneath her filthy shirt. "My Vernella don't live here," she said, "not now, she's in the halfway house again. Cinda's got her own place down to Friendship, but stops by a lot. She's got her own car now, a blue one, a Chevy. I think it's a Chevy. I don't know where Dickie is right now, he ain't been home for three days."

"So how many kids live here?"

"Dickie and Tina and Becca, that's all. Freddie died."

"This is Becca?"

"Oh yes, this is Becca, this is my Becca!" The silvery eyes went suddenly wide, showing jaundiced and blood-streaked whites. "She's Mama's darlin', ain't you honey? Mama's little doll." She stared at Steve, her mouth suddenly slack, then said, "Please don't take her away."

"I'm not here to take any children away," Steve said, "I'm here to talk about programs. If your income's low and you have dependents, you can get Aid for Needy Families."

Mrs. Taggart winced, as if in pain. "I had it before, it ain't much."

"I know. But your husband will also have to pay child support."

"He won't. Not Vernon, he ain't got no work."

"We'll see," Steve said, and wrote on his pad. "Do you know about SSI?"

"Lucille got it."

"Who's Lucille?"

"Down the Howard Road."

"Oh."

"Benny Turner got it. I think that was it. You get SSI if you're blind?"

"Yes. Blind, or over sixty-five, or disabled, if you don't have much income."

Mrs. Taggart laughed sharply, displaying her toothless and purple gums. The laugh faded quickly; she stared at the table again. "I got *no* income. None. I put my squash seeds in too early, they rotted. My punkins too. I got some lettuce comin' along, but you can't live on lettuce. My peas look okay."

Becca, with a wrinkled nose, pressed a thumb in the center of her Play-Doh. A black tray of biscuits sat on the range behind her. Above the range were shelves containing cans of fruits and vegetables, a box of wooden matches and some cans of paint. On the top shelf a picture of Jesus, curling, leaned against the wall.

"You go to the Social Security office and tell them you want to apply for SSI," Steve said. "Tell them you can't work because of your leg."

"An' it's true," Mrs. Taggart said. She held her right knee in her knobby hands. Her black basketball sneaker was ripped down the side and dirty flesh poked through. "Sometimes they don't believe you there, but it's true. An' not only my leg, but the spells. *I* call 'em the spells."

"What do you mean?" Steve said.

A tangle of cobwebs hung from the ceiling in looping strands and clots. The paint up there was black with soot from the rusty Franklin stove. On top of the chipped refrigerator, which stood beside the sink, was a basket of rags—or maybe it was the laundry. The rounded single door of the fridge was smudged with gray handprints. Some bills were pinned there by colorful magnets shaped like fruits.

Mrs. Taggart wrinkled her brow at the fridge as she said, "The spells? They just come over me. I take the pills. Not all the time, but most days I do. I can't help it, they just keep comin', and now with Vernon gone, I been takin' three. I used to take only one."

"What kind of pills?" Steve asked.

"Stelazine, it's called. Just a tiny little purple thing, but it sure is strong. Sometimes I sleep all day, like Vernella."

"Vernella's your oldest?"

Again Mrs. Taggart laughed. "I had her at nineteen, and now...I'm forty-two! You get old so fast."

Steve was thirty-four. It was hard to believe this woman was only eight years older than he was. He wrote on his pad.

The TV was showing commercials now, and Becca stopped kneading the Play-Doh and stared at the set. A truck was speeding down a twisting mountain road.

"So where's Vernella?" Steve asked.

"In the halfway house. They let her out a month ago, and she'd sleep all day and stay awake all night. Them drugs ate her brain. Her boyfriend's to blame, they was workin' over to Paradise Packin', he took her out to the car at lunch an' shot 'em right into her arm. She didn't know who she was for three days, my God what a time we had! I got four spells. That was two years ago. She's been in AMHI three times now. Last time she was home she took all the knives to the dump. Just emptied the drawers in a plastic bag an' took it all down to the dump. She said she was scared of the knives. She got all the spoons an' the forks, too, she got everything. She got my potato peeler. Dickie went down an' brought most of it back. One night I woke up at two o'clock an' found her just standin' right there at the foot of my bed. I go, 'What're you doin'?' She don't say nothin'. I ask her again, an' after a while she goes, 'I like to watch people sleep.' We had to send her back."

"Is she going to be coming home again?"

"Pretty soon, I guess. They don't keep 'em down there long. She's in Portland."

Steve nodded and wrote on his pad. "Well look, if you get SSI, you'll get Medicaid too. That'll pay all your doctor bills."

Mrs. Taggart sniffed, tossing her head back sharply. Her red hair, stiff as a brush, didn't move. "Doctors, well, they don't help much, you want my opinion. Vernella's got it."

"Got what?"

"SSI."

"Oh, right."

"Why she thinks little Becca is evil is what I don't get."

"What?"

"That's what she says, an' Becca is just the sweetest thing. Vernella has funny ideas sometimes."

Becca was sticking the chicken bones into the Play-Doh, making them stand straight up. Steve thought of the naked dead elm at the side of the road. One bone fell over; she righted it quickly. Behind her, a cat jumped onto the stove and sniffed at the pan of biscuits.

"Get down!" Mrs. Taggart yelled in a high-pitched screech. "Elvis! You stop that!"

The cat started eating a biscuit.

Shaking her head, Mrs. Taggart said, "They never listen, they never mind, you got to keep everything put away..." Her face went blank.

Becca glanced at Steve quickly again, then frowned at the Play-Doh.

"Another reason I'm here," Steve said, "is that Anne has certain concerns about Becca."

At this, Mrs. Taggart looked up, her eyes alarmed. "She's all I got!" she said. "You can't take her away, you can't!"

"I'm not going to take her away," Steve said.

Mrs. Taggart moaned. She held her head. "I'd work if I could," she said, "but you hurt your leg an' your rhythm's gone. You can't pack fish if your rhythm's gone." She slapped her hands on her thighs, and now she grinned. "I used to work next to Lena Hummer, fastest packer in Maine. You see her picture in the paper that time?"

"I don't think so," Steve said.

"Fastest packer in Maine! She rocked back an' forth so fast, that girl had rhythm! The governor gave her a big award. She's retired now."

"Uh-huh."

Mrs. Taggart's face fell. "Tina just won't mind what I say, she's as bad as the cats. And Dickie, I don't know where he is, him an' his pills."

"What pills?" Steve said.

"His powders an' pills. Not stelazine, but I know he's got somethin', he don't act right at times. It ain't real bad though, not like Vernella." She smiled abruptly, her dark gums gleaming. "But Becca's my little *darlin'*, she's a *good* girl, she *always* minds, don't you, dear?"

Becca thrust out her chin as she mashed the Play-Doh.

"Anne's mainly concerned that she never sees other kids," Steve said.

"She sees Tina."

"Other kids her own age."

Mrs. Taggart again clamped her hands on her head and shook it from side to side, her eyes looking up at the ceiling. "There ain't any on this road," she said, "not one. There used to be the Williams boy, but they moved to China. Musta been two years ago, I can't keep track of time." Her fingers still stuck in her patchy red hair, she started a high-pitched humming. Huge circles of sweat soaked her armpits.

Steve waited a minute, then said, "Mrs. Taggart?"

She kept on humming and holding her head, still looking up. The sound was a broken monotone as she started to rock back and forth. First it increased in volume and then in pitch. Becca pounded the Play-Doh briskly. The humming went higher, then stopped. Mrs. Taggart stopped rocking. She looked down and blinked.

"Anne's talked to you about kindergarten?" Steve asked quietly.

Mrs. Taggart stared, frowning, hands still on her head. Then she sniffed, sucking mucous back into her throat, and said in a cracked voice, "What?"

"Did Anne Collins talk to you about kindergarten?"

"Kindergarten?"

"For Becca—in the fall."

"Oh, in the *fall*," Mrs. Taggart said, looking concerned. She took her hands down, examined her knuckles, banged her fists together and said, "I don't want her to go."

"Why not?"

"Well that's the mistake I made with Tina, made her go too

soon. She was five, just like Becca'll be. I had to drag her onto the bus, she kicked and screamed, oh it was terrible. They said it would do her good, but it didn't. She never listens to me. She don't talk in school."

"Does Becca talk?"

Wide eyes again. "Oh, Becca talks *good.*" She grinned at the child and said, "You talk *good,* don't you, darlin'?"

Becca scowled at the table, her slender hands kneading the dough. The chicken bones had been shoved aside into a pile.

Steve moved one of his shoes. It came loose from the floor with a ripping sound.

"I give her a lot of toys," Mrs. Taggart said.

Steve glanced at the living room doorway: the box with the TV, the huge mound of broken dolls. The walls in that room were a dark bluegreen, and the plaster was bulging and cracked. A cream-colored lump of it lay on the rug.

"I can see that you do," Steve said, "but we think that it might be a good idea if Becca saw other kids too. She'd have fun with them, and learn to talk even better. Your library has a story hour on Wednesdays we think she'd enjoy."

"Car don't run," Mrs. Taggart said shaking her head. "If it did, I don't got the money for gas."

"We could get somebody to pick you up."

Mrs. Taggart inhaled quickly, twice; held the air in, then let it out hard in a rush. "I don't know," she said. "They don't have to go till they're seven, right?"

"To school."

"Yeah. I want her to be with me. I want her to be right here. I don't even let her out back because of the wildcats."

"Wildcats?"

"Dickie seen one out there."

"Wildcats on the coast of Maine?"

"Oh yes, Dickie seen one."

"Amazing," Steve said. "I met a guy last week who told me he saw a bear in St. George."

"Ha!" Mrs. Taggart said loudly. "A bear! I bet he did!"

Steve made a few notes. The cat jumped down from the stove, apparently full. The TV people were having big problems. "*This can't be happening!*" a woman screamed.

Mrs. Taggart stared out the picture window, past the ceramic cow with the broken tail that sat on the splintery sill. The cat started rubbing against her leg.

"I just can't stand to be alone," she said, staring off into space. "Vernon wasn't a man anymore once they took out that gland, but I loved him all the same. Life's no good without love, it's no good at all, makes you want..." She stopped; her right cheek twitched; and then in a voice that was almost inaudible: "Makes you want...to kill yourself."

Becca was up on her knees now, squashing her Play-Doh hard with the heel of her hand.

"Do you still see a doctor about your spells?" Steve asked.

"I ain't seen him in seven years," Mrs. Taggart said softly.

"Then how do you still get pills?"

"I just go to the drugstore an' get 'em."

"And how do you know how many to take?"

Mrs. Taggart kept staring outside. "If I'm feelin' good, I just take one...or maybe two. I can't take five, I sleep all day. Like Vernella."

"Maybe you ought to go back to the doctor again, it's been a long time."

"Yeah, maybe."

It occurred to Steve then that he must be unreal to this woman—like someone she'd see on TV. When he left this house he'd evaporate, like the soap opera people did when you switched off the set. "Do you have any questions?" he asked.

Mrs. Taggart said nothing.

"If not, I'm going now. Anne will be back in touch, and so will I. Do you need a ride to the Social Security office?"

"Agnes can take me."

"Okay. And you'll go to Human Services too and look into

Food Stamps and Aid to Needy Families?"

"I guess."

"Maybe I'll see you there," Steve said, getting up.

"Oh, is that where you work?" Mrs. Taggart said quickly, turning away from the window and frowning.

"Next door to Anne Collins."

A smile. "She's nice."

"She is," Steve said. "Bye, Becca."

The child's eyes flared for a second, then narrowed again. She bore down hard on her Play-Doh.

Steve let himself out. As he opened the door, Elvis darted between his legs. He noticed now that the bare dirt yard was covered with beer bottle caps.

∼

On the drive back to Human Services, Steve thought of the farm.

The apple tree in the Taggarts' yard had reminded him of it, that tree with the tire. A tire had hung from a tree on the farm all the years he had played there. Grampop Hillman had hung that tire, and Steve and his sister had swung on it every visit, till they got too big.

When Steve was a kid, his parents went to the farm several times each summer. The place was a paradise, with its fields rolling down to the water's edge, its huge cow barn with its loft full of hay, its view of the islands and coves with their clusters of boats. Steve swam off the dock and caught mackerel and pollock and played with the collie, Champ, in those meadows lush with with daisies and blackeyed Susans. There were wild fruits: lowbush blueberries, raspberries, blackberries, wild tart apples that Grammom Hillman made into pies and applesauce.

When his grandparents died twelve years ago, Steve's parents sold the farm. The town had already gone through some major changes, was well on its way to being transformed from a quiet Maine village into a bustling outlet center like hundreds of others anywhere. The farm's taxes doubled in just eight years,

Steve's parents couldn't afford them and sold the place.

Three years ago Steve had stopped in that town to look for a sweater when, on a whim, he left the business district, drove down the street that led to the farm, ascended the hill, crossed the railroad tracks—and to his amazement the place was still there. The buildings were rundown and empty, but all still there—waiting for a developer to make his move. Steve had walked through the tangled field to the water's edge, and there was the tree, with that same old tire hanging on its darkened, thick, frayed rope. His sadness had overwhelmed him then, and he'd quickly left, and he knew he would never go back there again.

～

Anne Collins looked up from her desk. Its mottled gray top was piled with papers and folders, all neatly stacked. "Well, what do you think?" she said.

"Her comprehension seems okay," Steve said, "but I'd have to see her again to know for sure."

"So you're going back."

"I think I should."

"Maybe we can go together."

"Good idea," Steve said. "You can help me fight off the wildcats."

"She told you that story too," Anne said.

Steve laughed.

A breeze brought the sweet smell of freshly cut grass through the window. The pale green paint below the sill had started to flake away, revealing the plaster, making Steve think of the Taggarts' living room wall. He said: "What about Child Protective?"

Anne tilted her head with a frown. She had dark red hair, gray eyes, pale freckled skin. Her shoulders were solid and broad. "Do you think it's that bad?"

"I don't know, I'm just worried," Steve said. "The way the mother went out into space like that..."

"She's a weird one, all right. But Child Protective, what

would you want them to do?"

"Just look into the situation, I guess. The woman pops pills whenever she wants to."

"I know, but Child Protective deals with the hard core stuff."

"You don't think we should bother?"

"I don't think we'll get anywhere. There are thirty-five thousand reports of child abuse in this state every year, and fewer than ten percent are investigated. It's all they have time for. This doesn't sound like a critical situation."

"I'd still like to give it a try."

"Lots of luck."

"The kid didn't say a word," Steve said, "but I think she's bright. She sure is pretty."

"So's Tina. She's already in fifth grade and she never talks. She does average work, but she never talks."

"I don't think we're going to get very far with kindergarten."

"Maybe not. Maybe we'll try a home teacher first. What's next week's schedule look like?"

"Let me get my book."

$\sim$

After he set up the time with Anne, he went downstairs to the waiting room. In his almost two years at Human Services, he'd never dealt with Child Protective before. The receptionist, Laura, put in a call to "Wendy." A few minutes later a sad-looking woman of forty or so came out to meet him.

He followed her into a huge space lighted by bright fluorescents. They sat at her desk and he voiced his concerns.

"Are there signs of actual abuse?"

"It's more neglect," Steve said.

"No signs of being beaten? She seems to be healthy?"

"I guess so. She's dirty, *really* dirty. I bet she hasn't had a bath in months."

Wendy shrugged her thin shoulders. "Anne Collins can deal with that. The kids we deal with are really *abused*."

"I know. I just feel something really bad could happen here. Most of the time, the kid must take care of herself, her mother's out in space. And there's serious drinking going on, the yard's full of beer bottle caps."

"I'll put her name on my list," Wendy said, "but I can't tell you when I'll get over there."

Steve let out a breath. "Her older sister's pretty disturbed," he said, "been in AMHI a couple of times. She's in a halfway house right now, but'll come home soon. She thinks Becca is 'evil.'"

"Huh," Wendy said, and wrote on her pad. "How old's this sister?"

"Early twenties."

"I'll put the kid on my list."

~

He got home after six. Another ten hour day.

Karen was lying back on the living room couch looking weary and pale, her head on a pillow.

Steve sat beside her and took her hand. "Still bad," he said.

"Oh God," she said.

"Did you have to leave early again?"

She shook her head. "I stuck it out, but at one point I almost puked on a manuscript."

"Jesus."

"Maybe I shouldn't keep taking the pills."

Steve shrugged. "But maybe it's not the pills, you felt rotten during the other pregnancies too."

"This is worse," Karen said. She ran three fingers across her forehead, wiping away the sweat. "Another eight months of this?"

"It'll pass," Steve said. "It passed the other times. I think you should stay on the pills."

"I guess so," Karen said, and blew out a breath.

"Are you going to want any dinner?"

"What are you making?"

"Spaghetti."

"Oh God."

"We could just have some noodles. Plain noodles."

"Later, maybe."

"I'm hungry. I'm going to make some."

"I might have some later."

He kissed her forehead. "It isn't fair. Four years of this nonsense, and other couples have babies without even trying."

"Not all of them. Not Jack and Marcie."

"No, but they finally had one."

"Yes," she said, "and we will too, this time it's going to work. It's got to work."

"It will," Steve said, and squeezed her hand.

She smiled weakly. "How was your day?"

"Disturbing," Steve said. "I went to see a kid in Welshboro, four year old girl who doesn't talk. Well, maybe she does, we'll see, she didn't while I was there. Her mother's on Stelazine, really disturbed. She's forty-two and looks twenty years older."

"Some people lead such hard lives."

"She cut up her leg with a chainsaw, can't work, her husband just left her, she has no money... The kid is gorgeous, beautiful."

"You fell in love with her."

"Of course."

"You always fall in love with them."

"I can't help it."

"It's not professional."

"I know."

"Give me a kiss."

He did, then looked at her golden eyes. "We'd like to get her around other kids," he said, "but it's going to be hard."

"I guess," Karen said. She looked away, across the room. "I went to the store after work and this woman was there with an Asian child. She must've been three, maybe three and a half. She talked up a storm. Adorable."

Steve kissed her again and she said, "I shouldn't be

envious."

"You're entitled."

"Who knows what that woman's been through?"

"Who knows?" Steve said. He stood. "I'm going to change my clothes. You want something to drink? Coke or something?"

"Not right now, maybe later."

~

In the bedroom, Steve thought about Becca Taggart: kept seeing her there at the greasy table, pushing the Play-Doh hard with the heels of her hands, averting her eyes when he looked her way. Unable to talk? Or simply unwilling? He wondered about her view of the world, her view of people, and thought: *If she lived here with us she'd be so different...*

He hung up his slacks and looked at the painting beside the closet, roses in a dark blue vase, the work of an old friend, Gloria James. Gloria had given it to them four years ago, soon after the birth of her daughter.

Four years ago. Years of worry and waiting and tests that were painful, embarrassing, costly and inconclusive. Twice, Karen had gotten pregnant. They hadn't told anyone, scared it would ruin their luck; had ridden the roller coaster high for weeks, had decided on names—Mark for a boy, Julia for a girl—then plunged to the terrible depths.

The second time, the pregnancy lasted for almost three months. They had been on the brink of telling their parents the joyful news when the bleeding began. Karen was violently ill for two days and her arms went numb. She saw a psychologist twice and began going back to church.

All of their married friends had children. Even Marcie, who'd struggled for years to have her first, had just gotten pregnant again. Karen was almost thirty-three, and time was an enemy now. The pressure was building. The comments of parents and friends had begun to cut deeper. At dinner last weekend Steve's mother had said, "I read in the paper the other day how the chances of having a handicapped child increase the older you get." Karen's mother, a month ago, on the phone: "If I could do everything over again, I'd have my children earlier." *Enough*, Steve wanted to say, *the fact of the matter is, we have a problem,* but he hadn't been able to say it.

He had pretty much made up his mind: if it didn't work out this time, they would try to adopt. The tests, the planning, the pain, the failures had frayed their nerves—and had totally ruined sex. They slept together for only one reason: hope. No excitement, no joy. They wished it could be otherwise, but temperature charts and saving up sperm and having to "make love" on certain days were too much to overcome.

Adoption, Steve said to himself as he put on his jeans. Now what are you thinking about *that* for? Think positive thoughts, okay? This new medication will do it. The sickness will pass pretty soon and the pills will work, *believe* it. Excited, he made a fist, then told himself: *Calm down, don't get carried away, take it easy, one day at a time.* He fastened his belt and put on his shoes and went down to make some dinner.

∾

Karen ate nothing and went to bed early. Worried, Steve drank bourbon and watched the news.

A story about homeless children in Rio came on. The boys the reporter interviewed were black and bronze, they ranged in age from five to nine, wore nothing but filthy torn shorts and survived by stealing. As they talked to the camera, they passed around plastic bags of glue, inhaling greedily. They had sleepy dazed looks on their faces, their speech was slurred, they staggered with rolled-back eyes. The reporter said no one in government had any plans to help them. Thinking of Child Protective and Wendy, Steve hit the button and turned off the set. The image of Rio's homeless boys blended into the image of Becca Taggart, and he had bad dreams.

∾

Anne drove. She had an old Subaru four wheel drive wagon. Its back seat was filled with boxes and large manila envelopes.

As always in Maine, spring had taken an age to arrive. Now, as if to make up for lost time, the heat had come on in a rush. Yesterday had been sunny and sixty-two; today was overcast, but close to eighty.

Steve was wearing a shortsleeve shirt without any tie, but he still felt hot; there was sweat on his nose. "Wendy something," he said.

"Wendy Lassiter," Anne said.

"That's it."

"So what did she say?"

"She doesn't think it sounds that serious."

Anne flipped the sun visor down as she said, "I thought that would be her reaction. I work with this boy who was really abused, a two year old. I mean cigarette burns, the whole nine yards, so they put him in foster care for three months, now he's back with the mother again. It kills me, this woman is just not ready." Anne squinted against the glare and shook her head. "She's been through drug rehab, she's in AA, but she's just not ready to care for a child again. She's so full of anger and hate..."

They were passing a dark red trailer that Steve hadn't noticed the last time he'd come. Its hedge had the pale tight beginnings of leaves. "Most of the time you hear that they take kids away at the drop of a hat," he said.

"They will if there's clear abuse," Anne said. "They took this little fellow away real fast, but they sent him back fast too. Too fast." She shrugged. "There's a whole lot of pressure on them to keep kids at home with their natural parents."

"I know," Steve said.

The dog was not chained to its stake and the brown car was gone. Anne pulled the Subaru into the potholed dooryard and turned off the key. They reached in the back and picked up their briefcases, opened their doors and got out of the car.

The puddle beside the dirt path to the cape's front door had shrunk dramatically. A red piece of plastic was stuck in its mud. The apple tree with the tire swing was showing fat buds, and tiger grass was sprouting beside the cape's rough stone foundation.

Tiger grass. Steve remembered that time in graduate school. His first spring in Pennsylvania he said to some classmates, "Tiger grass up already. In *March*." They looked at him oddly, and one of them said, "Tiger lilies, you mean?" "We call it tiger grass in Maine," he said. "Maine must be a weird place," a girl named Janine said. "Tiger grass." Janine was black, and to Steve she had seemed exotic.

He knocked on the door. The window pane rattled. They waited. Next to the granite slab that served as a doorstep the brown Christmas wreath lay, spattered with mud. A plastic trike with a missing front wheel was snagged in the tiger grass under the picture window.

The TV was on in there, Steve could hear it. He knocked again. From where he stood, he could see through the far right side of the picture window. A steaming mug sat on the table. A cat appeared—not Elvis, it wasn't black—sniffed at the mug, ate something beside it and jumped away. Then the dog started barking behind the door.

Again Steve knocked. The dog barked louder. When it quieted down, Anne called out, "Vera?"

The dog started barking again. They waited.

A tiny insect darted in front of Steve's eyes. He waved it off, hitting the side of his glasses.

"Black flies," Anne said. "Spring is here."

Steve straightened his glasses. "I'm allergic to them. Natives are supposed to be immune, but not this native. One little bite is all it takes to blow me up like a balloon." He knocked on the door. "Come on, Mrs. Taggart," he said in a soft voice, and batted the air again.

Anne smacked her ear. "I guess we struck out," she said.

They went to the car, swatting the insects, hurried inside and rolled up the windows. As Anne pulled away, Steve said,

"They're obviously home."

"Hiding out," Anne said. "I get a lot of that."

~

They came into Human Services through the back door, the Elm Street entrance, and down at the other end of the hallway they heard someone scream in the waiting room: "In *custody?* My kid? Over my dead *body* you are." There was silence, and then: "The *fuck* you are!"

Anne rolled her eyes and looked at Steve and said in a quiet voice, "I wouldn't work for Child Protective no matter how much you paid me."

They went upstairs. Steve set his briefcase next to his desk, then went to the window, looked at the parking lot. A scrawny blond-haired woman was twirling a pair of silver-lensed glasses around and around in her hand. "Fuck all of you!" she yelled. As he watched her get in her car, Steve thought: *What the hell am I doing here?*

~

Steve was convinced that much of his life had been ruled by chance. He'd entered college as a drama major, had taken required foundation courses in speech, had met speech pathology majors. He hadn't known a thing about that field before he met these people. While talking with them, he suddenly realized that here was a way he could make ends meet while he looked for work in the theater.

He had never had any burning desire to help other people, but once he got into his practicum, in his senior year, he started to see the world in a different light. The theater majors were going around in overcoats with hems that swept the ground and oversized mufflers around their necks, striking poses and polishing phony accents, while he was studying brain disorders, language disorders, semantics, linguistics— things that were *real.* He abandoned the world of artifice and swollen egos, went for his master's degree at a different school, and never told anyone there that he'd once loved the stage.

Except Karen, after they'd gone to see a campus production of *Endgame*. They'd met by chance. A guy he barely knew had dragged him to a party and there she was, with her auburn hair and golden eyes. They struck up a conversation, talked all night, and he asked her out. She was a senior, in journalism. After they saw the play, on their second date, he said, "I started out as a drama major, but realized I just didn't like that world." "Why not?" she asked, those beautiful eyes on his. He shrugged. "Even when it's supposed to be real, it's fake."

They married right after he graduated, and moved to Maine, where he took a job in a clinic for handicapped children. Five years later (by chance—the clinic director abruptly resigned) he was helping to run the place. Then the job expanded, and after a few more years he was no longer doing therapy, just administrative work, and now he had this case coordinator job. He'd started college intent on becoming an actor, and ended up being a bureaucrat.

That's how things went for most people, he thought. In college he'd known a few students who'd set out to be accountants or dentists or teachers and that's what they were today, but for most of the people he knew, a door had come open, they'd crossed the threshold, and found themselves in a place they had never imagined, a place that would claim them for years, perhaps for life.

The way he'd gone back to acting—another accident. A woman who worked in Adult Protective had mentioned how hard it was to recruit for the local civic theater. When Steve showed an interest, she said that he ought to audition, and once he was up on the stage with a script in his hand, there it was, the old thrill. He was given the lead, and everyone told him he did an outstanding job. In bed with the rush of the stage still hot in his blood the night of the first performance, he lay awake thinking about his life. He stared at the doorway, the walls with their dark squares of paintings, the ceiling, the black light fixture, and couldn't sleep till dawn.

Things just happened. You went down the road and here was a detour, you took it, and here was another detour, another, another... Before you knew it, the detours became your life. You looked around and asked yourself: *How did I get here? How did I ever become this person, doing the things I do?*

∽

Karen still wasn't feeling well. Steve made her some tea and toast, then fixed a grilled cheese sandwich for himself. He had a beer and watched the news while Karen rested in bed. Later, lying beside her, he said, "If I hadn't gone to graduate school— if I hadn't gone to that *party*—I'd never have met you."

"And you'd probably have a dozen kids by now."

This startled him. He said, "I didn't mean that, I meant I was lucky."

"But now you're not."

"Of course I am. With you, I'll always be lucky."

She shook her head. "We can't have children."

"We will," he said. "We'll be lucky with that too, wait and see." He kissed her cheek. She sighed and turned away and tried to sleep.

She was restless all night, and Steve was too. In his dreams he kept seeing that cat on the Taggarts' table.

∽

He called their number at nine fifteen the next morning. The phone rang seven times before a hoarse dull voice said, "Yeah?"

"Is Mrs. Taggart there?"

"Hold on."

He waited. Crackling sounds, and then Mrs. Taggart's piercing high voice said, "Hello?"

"Hi, this is Steve Hillman from Human Services. We had an appointment yesterday but nobody answered the door when I knocked. I'm going to be down your way again in a little while, you mind if I stop by?"

A silence. Steve waited. "Mrs. Taggart?"

"You want to stop by?"

"If it's okay with you."

"It's okay, I guess."

"Good. I'll see you in about an hour."

"Okay." Another pause. "Is it warm where you are?"

"It sure is."

"Where are you again?"

"In Limerock. Human Services."

"Oh, yeah. Warm." Crackling sounds again, then: "I just made some biscuits, and *they're* sure warm."

"Uh-huh," Steve said. "I'll see you soon."

"Okay."

Steve hung up the phone, put some things in his briefcase, and went downstairs. In the waiting room, a girl who looked about fourteen was sitting slumped forward, biting her nails. Beside her chair, in an infant seat, sat a tiny baby, crying.

～

Mrs. Taggart was out by the mangled mailbox, inspecting an unopened envelope. Becca played in the dirt with a fork and a blue plastic dish. As soon as she saw Steve's car, she bolted behind the house. The dog, on its chain again, showed its teeth and began to bark.

Steve parked in the dooryard, picked up his briefcase, got out of the car. He'd wanted to come with Anne again, but she was too busy.

Paying him no attention at all, Mrs. Taggart started to walk toward the house, scowling at the mail in her hand and muttering something.

"Hi," Steve said.

At the doorway she stopped and turned, squinting sharply. "Oh, hi," she said in a soft flat voice. She was wearing the same clothes she'd worn last time.

A black fly danced at Steve's eyes and he brushed it away, then followed Mrs. Taggart inside. She left the glass-paned door wide open. There was no screen door. "Warm," she said. She stared at the envelope in her hand, then dropped it onto the tablecloth. It hit on its long edge, coming to rest near a stick of margerine, soft and smeared in its rumpled wrapper. She gingerly sat in the chair she had sat in before and frowned at the envelope. Its return address was that of the district court.

Setting his briefcase on the floor, Steve sat. The stench was thick in the muggy heat. A fly with a green back, fat and shiny, lit on the margerine. "I came with Anne Collins yesterday," Steve said, "but she couldn't make it today. We wanted to talk to you about several things—the library story hour, kindergarten—"

"He ain't comin' back!" Mrs. Taggart said, her voice a loud high wail. Then she buried her face in her hands and started to weep.

Steve wondered where Becca was. High up on the wooden box in the next room, a game show was winding down. A large black woman had guessed a word and won twenty-five thousand dollars.

Mrs. Taggart sucked desperate gulps of air, wiping her soggy eyes with her grimy hands. "Just as well," she said. She looked at the window a minute, then back at the table, the envelope. "Just as well," she repeated. "Touchin' them in their secret places."

"What?" Steve said.

"Took all his tools," Mrs. Taggart said. She bit some loose skin off her knuckle and spat it out onto the floor.

Steve reached in his briefcase and took out his pad. "Last time I was here, you told me how Tina won't listen to what you say? There's a teacher could come here and help you with that if you want."

Mrs. Taggart kept frowning hard at the table. Running her hand through her knots of red hair and blinking her bruised-looking eyelids she said in a soft voice, "Child Protective." She started to hum, baring her toothless gums.

On the TV, the audience screamed. "Just a teacher," Steve said, "not Child Protective," and Mrs. Taggart tilted her head back, humming louder, eyes closed tight. Steve sat and waited. After a minute he said, "Mrs. Taggart?"

The humming stopped. Mrs. Taggart looked up at him out of the sides of her eyes. A cat came in through the open door and rubbed against her leg. She seemed not to notice.

"A concern that Anne and I have," Steve said, "is we never hear Becca talk."

"She talks real good!" Mrs. Taggart said, her eyes suddenly fierce. "I already told you that, didn't I? Didn't I tell you that?" She stood up abruptly and went through the door where the TV stood. Steve looked at the mountain of mangled dolls, the fur and plaster dust on the scalloped rug, the hole in the wall. He heard thumping sounds, then a short high squeal, then he saw Mrs. Taggart's back, her torn and soiled shirt and pants, then saw that she had Becca's arms and was pulling her hard. He saw the child's shoeless feet, those dirt-caked ankles and toes, skidding over the mangy rug. "You talk for the man!" Mrs. Taggart said. "Come out here an' talk for the man!"

The child fought violently, kicking her mother's shins. Mrs. Taggart let go. "Well maybe Vernella's right!" she yelled. "Maybe you *are* the devil!"

She came back to the kitchen, laughing. "She talks real good, Becca does, but she's kinda shy. Oh my can she kick! Did you see her kick? She got my leg, my bad one, I need some aspirin." She turned toward the doorway. "Becca! Come out here! Come out here an' talk for the man!" She sighed and made a clucking sound and said, "She won't mind, she's a little devil. You devil!"

She sat at the table again, breathing hard. "Vernon got emphysema. Smoked too many cigarettes, the kind without filters. Well he done a lotta bad things, it's best he's gone, but the love... I miss the love..."

Her tears welled up again, and Steve had a frightening thought: of that Child Protective worker accused of having sex with a client's mother. The guy had been cleared of all charges, but even so, his defense had cost him thousands of dollars, and nobody ever trusted him again. Steve thought: *This woman is right on the edge, she could suddenly snap and accuse me of something like that, and how could I prove she was lying?* He started to sweat. Maybe she really believed there *were* wildcats out in her yard. Maybe she actually *saw* them.

Mrs. Taggart stopped crying and said, looking up with bright eyes, "I love my girls. Tina done the most beautiful pitcher in school," and then she was up again, into the next room again. Steve heard her talking away to herself, and soon she returned with a crayon sketch that was spotted and smudged and torn. Pushing aside the sugar bowl, she spread the drawing out. Steve looked at it: a girl with a giant head and a mouth full of pointed teeth. "See, ain't that good?" Mrs. Taggart said. "Tina watches TV."

"It's very good," Steve said.

"I love my girls."

"I know you do, and I'm sure you want to do the best you can for them. That's why I think this teacher should visit. She'll help you to do your best."

"It's hard," Mrs. Taggart said. "I try, but it's hard, when you don't have no money, you don't have no car, your husband runs off an' your leg's no good. I'd work if I could. It's too hard with my leg."

"I know, but there's help. Have you gone to Social Security yet?"

"Don't have no car."

"I thought you could get a ride."

"From who?"

"You told me you had a friend."

"You mean Agnes?"

"Yeah, that was her name."

"She got sick. Had her gallbladder out."

"I can give you a ride, then."

She narrowed her eyes. "Well Dickie says he can give me a ride, but he's busy now."

"If he can't help, Anne or I can take you."

"Oh? Oh, maybe...I don't know..."

She tossed her head and rolled her eyes and started to hum again. As Steve wrote on his pad, he saw movement off to his right. He looked up.

A huge puffy-faced, pale-skinned woman stood in the doorway in front of the box full of dolls. Strands of greasy black hair hung down over her ears. She was wearing a pair of black shorts and a black tank top with "Leader of the Pack" across it in red. Her shoulders were dark with tattoos and her feet were bare. "What the hell's all that goddamn noise?" she yelled in a gravelly voice. "Did I tell you I wanted to sleep?"

Mrs. Taggart was humming louder now, and rocking back and forth.

"Goddamn you!" the fat woman said. "I'll kill that fuckin' brat, I swear to God!" With a sneer on her face, she turned and lashed out at the dolls with a naked foot. Three of them hit the wall, and one of the heads snapped off. A thick chunk of plaster landed beside the head. "That goddamn brat!" the woman screamed, and disappeared.

Mrs. Taggart was making a gasping sound.

"You okay?" Steve said.

And now she was wheezing, her chest heaving hard. "Vernella," she said between wheezes, and picked up the envelope there on the tablecloth, blinking and shaking her head. "Vernella."

Buicks were being sold on TV. Mrs. Taggart sat motionless, staring down: at her hands, at the envelope.

"Maybe I better come back some other time," Steve said.

Mrs. Taggart seemed not to hear.

"I'll come back some other time," Steve said.

~

Thumbing through her monthly minder, Wendy Lassiter said, "No openings for two weeks."

"Maybe somebody else can do it, then?" Steve was standing

in front of her desk, which was deluged with papers.

"Not a chance," Wendy said. "We're short of staff, Bill's leaving us."

A cluster of people stood near the back wall, talking and joking around. A coffee urn sat on a table there, next to a flat white rectangular cake decorated with pink and green.

"Which one's Bill?" Steve asked.

"The bald one, the one with the big moustache. He's been here two years. That's just about average. He's going to Voc Rehab. Nice work if you can get it."

Steve watched a tall redhaired guy eat some cake. He looked back at Wendy and said, "She told me her husband touched them in secret places."

Raising her eyebrows, Wendy shrugged. "Yeah, most of them say that kind of stuff. They're pissed at their husbands, they say it to get them in trouble. They know what we want to hear. They know what works."

"Somehow I believe Mrs. Taggart."

"Why, if she's so disturbed?"

"I don't think she said it to get him in trouble, it just slipped out."

"People say anything," Wendy said. "Believe me, I've heard it all. She could say something bad about you too, you know, if she thinks you're a threat."

"I've thought of that."

"It's best to go there with somebody else."

"I'll do that next time—if there is a next time."

Wendy looked at her notes. "So the husband's out of the house. For good?"

"So Mrs. Taggart says. But her oldest daughter's back, and she's really scary. I think she may really believe that her sister's the devil."

A woman laughed across the room where the celebrants were. The bald-headed man sliced more cake, smiling broadly. At the desk next to Wendy's, a young woman spoke on the phone. "Did you call the police?" she said.

"I'll get there as soon as I can," Wendy said, "but not for at least two weeks. I've got three court appearances, I just don't have the time."

~

Karen miscarried the following evening, right before dinner. She was sick all night.

Steve stayed home the next morning, made her some tea and she slept. When he went to the bedroom to check on her, she was sitting against the headboard, cheeks wet with tears, face pale.

"It's not going to work," she said.

He sat on the edge of the bed and held her close, running his hand through her hair. "I think we should try to adopt," he said.

"It's so hard to adopt. There just aren't enough babies."

"There are—they're just not in Maine."

She wiped at her eyes with her fingers. He gave her a tissue. She used it to blow her nose. "I'm so damn sick of saying goodbye to Mark and Julia," she said.

"Let's try to adopt."

"I guess so. I just don't know. I guess so." She covered her eyes with her hand. "I wish we'd never bought this house. These empty bedrooms... Every time I walk through the hall I feel like a failure."

"No," he said, and held her again. "Maybe we'll go somewhere this weekend—if you feel okay."

"I'll *make* myself feel okay," she said. She wiped her eyes again.

He looked at the floor. "Would you ever consider foster care?"

She shook her head. "No, never, it's just too hard. To get attached to a child and then have to give it up..."

"But sometimes the foster parents adopt the kids."

"Not often, I bet."

"Not often, no, but it happens."

She chewed her lip. He waited a minute, then said, "Do you want more tea?"

She shook her head again. "No thanks." She closed her eyes and said, "I think it was Julia this time."

~

Steve couldn't eat anything either. He went to his office at one o'clock and did some paperwork. Most of his job consisted of filling out forms and writing plans. He sent this stuff to his supervisor, who looked it over and sent it on to the feds. If the paperwork was done correctly, the feds were satisfied; they never went into the field to check on cases. Steve could invent these children, submit pure fictions, and the feds would never know.

Today he couldn't concentrate. He kept thinking of Karen, and sometimes of Becca Taggart. He looked out the window, stared at the lilac bush starting to bloom at the edge of the parking lot, and wondered about the worth of this job of his.

When he visited families or schools, he felt he was doing something, like back in his old speech therapy days. But direct service jobs like that were too frustrating, too exhausting. He'd banged his head against that wall for seven years, and enough was enough.

He was putting things in his briefcase, preparing to leave the office, when the telephone rang.

The voice on the other end of the line said, "This is Joe Bevans. My little girl's goin' blind an' needs laser treatments in Boston an' I can't get her there. My truck's broke down an' I ain't got the money to pay nobody to take her. I tried the Social Security office, the Salvation Army, the Lions Club, Red Cross, the Shriners, nobody can help."

"Your child's not getting SSI," Steve said.

"They told us we make too much money."

"Well I can only pay for kids who receive disability checks."

"So you don't care either."

"It isn't a matter of caring," Steve said, "it's—"

"My kid's goin' blind, and nobody cares." the man said, his voice rising. "Nobody! She don't get this laser she's blind, and nobody gives a shit!"

Steve took a deep breath and said, "What about Medical Eye Care? They won't be able to pay for this trip, it takes a few weeks to process your application, but future trips—"

"They told me I make too much money," the man said. "Look, all I want is a Medicaid card so I can get down to Boston. I don't need money to pay for the treatments, I got Blue Cross, all I want is a *ride*. Is that too much to ask for? A Medicaid card?"

"You wouldn't think so," Steve began, "but you see—"

"But you *see*," the man mimicked, cutting him off. "Is that what you're gonna tell me? But you *see*? You're just like all the rest of them, you don't give a good goddamn if my kid goes blind! These goddamn welfare bums sit around on their asses all day an' get benefits, and me an' my wife both work and we don't get nothin'."

"I'm sorry," Steve said, "I know—"

"Oh, do you?" the man said. "You think you *know*? Is it your little girl who's goin' blind? You don't know shit!"

Steve's anger flared up in a sudden rush. His hand was tight on the phone and his mind was hot.

The line was silent. Finally Steve said, "Are you ready to listen now?"

"It seems like *you* ain't ready to listen to *me!*" the man shouted. "I thought people like you were supposed to care about kids, but you don't! You don't even care if my kid goes *blind!*"

Steve suddenly found that he couldn't speak. He put the receiver down on his desk and got up and went to the window.

He stared at the parking lot and his heart was pounding, thundering in his ears. *Jesus Christ,* he thought, *calm down, you'll die, you'll have a heart attack!* He stared at the lilac, barely aware of it, barely aware of the rows of parked cars.

Calm down, calm down, he told himself as his heart banged on. *This is stupid, for Christ's sake, stop it!*

When Steve cooled off enough to return to the phone, he expected to find it dead, but no, the man's mother was there. She apologized for her son's behavior, explaining that he was very upset, then ran through the whole situation again. Steve asked for the name of the child's doctor and said he would check to see if anyplace closer than Boston could do the laser.

The doctor returned his call two hours later, at five thirty-five, and told him the child had perfect sight in her healthy eye and wasn't in any danger of going blind. She did need to go to Boston, yes, but her mother—who lived apart from the father—had already set this up. And the Lions had already given the family money.

As Steve drove home, wrung out, he remembered his pounding heart as he'd stood at the window, staring, his mind on fire. It wasn't the first time he'd taken that kind of abuse in his job, but he'd never reacted so strongly before, never lost it like that before. Maybe, he thought, he'd gone down the human services road as far as he wanted to go.

∽

He never told Karen about that call, never talked about changing jobs. She had more than enough to think about without that. She slept well that night with his arms around her and felt much better the following morning.

While Steve was at work, she called some adoption agencies. The first two had waiting lists three years long. The third place didn't talk about years, and she made an appointment with them.

The weekend was windy and wet and they didn't go anywhere. Steve kept fretting about the appointment. What if the agency turned them down, or told them they'd have to wait forever? He thought of those classified ads he had seen. Would they come to that soon? The begging mode? He composed an ad in his head: *We are college graduates, very white, idyllically married and rolling in money. Won't you please, please help us build our family through adoption?*

They went to a movie on Sunday night, a comedy, which did them both good. On the ride back home they discussed adoption again. The movie's effect wore off and they soon fell silent.

The wipers were a metronome as Karen stared through the windshield. She yawned and looked suddenly tired. *Tired and thin,* Steve thought. Too thin, he would have to make sure she was eating enough. He said, "Want to stop at the Dairy Queen?"

"I'm not hungry," she said, and the silence descended again.

When they reached the house, Steve said, "I saw this program on Rio the other night."

She looked exhausted. "Oh?"

"It's loaded with homeless kids. They pick people's pockets, get high on glue, do anything to survive. Does this agency deal with South American kids?"

"I don't know."

"There are thousands of them without any families."

"All I want is one," Karen said.

~

That night he dreamed of a cafeteria. The line was moving terribly slowly, and he was extremely hungry. The lights that warmed the food were bright and hot, and bothered his eyes. He could barely see well enough to make his selection: baked chicken, potatoes, some carrots, some beans...

He looked off into the dining room where hundreds of people were eating, and there was Becca, alone at a table. *Where's Karen?* he thought. *Why is Becca alone, and why is she dirty again?* She was filthy: her hair was matted and dull, her T-shirt was stained, her feet were black with grime. Why had Karen allowed this to happen? And where had she gone?

The people ahead of him chose desserts, pulled levers for drinks, all terribly slowly, as if they'd been drugged. They had coppery skin and spoke Spanish. Not Spanish, no...Portuguese?

Come on, come on, Steve thought, *speed it up, I don't have the rest of my life to spend in this goddamn place, I'm already thirty-four!* He looked at his plate and his chicken was nothing but bones.

When he looked at the dining room again, Becca was gone. In a panic he left his tray and pushed past the people in line. As he hurried by, the cashier shouted some angry words in the foreign tongue. Steve went into the dining room.

And it wasn't a dining room now but a stage, a huge stage burning with spotlights. He hurried across its varnished boards and found himself at the edge of a dump, a dump filled with glittering kitchenware: knives, forks, spoons, ladles, salt and pepper shakers...

Far away at the foot of the mountain of refuse lay broken dolls. Their arms and legs stuck up at odd angles, their heads were twisted, they wore no clothes. Then one of the dolls started moving. It stuck its thin arm in the air, its fingers outstretched, grasping, and turned its head. With horror Steve saw it was Becca. He woke up soaking with sweat, and his heart was aching.

~

The week was filled with the annual flood of pupil evaluation meetings. Steve drove from school to school, averaging over a hundred miles a day. The weather was perfect, with brilliant skies and everything starting to bloom. It was great to be out of the office, away from the paperwork; great to be talking with people, to actually see the kids he wrote reports about.

His last meeting on Wednesday concerned a child he'd never seen before. She was eight and lived in a boarding home. Her mother lived two hundred miles away. To Steve's surprise, she showed up at the meeting.

The woman was maybe thirty, thin and attractive. Divorced. Unable to care for her child at home, since she worked full time. As she spoke, her daughter slumped in her wheelchair, her head to the side, a cord of drool extending from chin to shoulder.

"They think it might have been the pills I took," the mother said. "I couldn't get pregnant, they gave me these pills..."

~

The next afternoon Steve left work early, picked up Karen, drove to the adoption agency.

The place was in Lewiston, forty-five minutes away, in a big old converted house with a glassed-in porch. The social worker, a woman about their age, was pleasant enough, but Steve resented her questions.

Back in the car he said, "It looks like we have to be damn near perfect."

"It's not that bad," Karen said.

"We've been happily married eleven years," Steve said, "we've never committed a criminal act, we're both employed, we own a house—what more do they want? Why do we have to explore our feelings about having children—or not having children? We've already done that on our own."

"We'll do fine. They'll accept us, don't worry."

"I guess. It just irks me. I hate to have people pry into my life."

"Well, that's how it is."

"Yeah." He started the car and thought of the Taggarts, pictured himself taking notes at their kitchen table. "So no South American kids."

"No foreign kids. That surprised me, it seems so limiting."

"I'll say."

Steve pulled into the street. "It kills me. All those kids in Rio that nobody wants, that the country would like to get *rid* of, but can you get one? No. Does that make sense?"

"So now you're expecting life to make sense?"

He looked at her then and loved her with all his heart. "I'm glad we're doing this," he said.

She smiled. "Me too."

~

On Sunday, while he planted his garden, Steve thought of Mrs. Taggart. Even with all her problems, she'd gotten her garden in early—too early, in fact, her squash seeds had rotted—but here he was planting peas at the end of May.

Karen came home from church with the Sunday paper. They sat at the table with coffee and bagels and read it, and suddenly Steve said, "Jesus."

Karen looked up. "What's wrong?"

"The brother of that girl I told you about? That beautiful girl with the crazy mother I went to see a couple of weeks ago? He was picked up for selling cocaine."

"Oh, great."

"The mother said she thought he was doing drugs, and I told the Child Protective worker. You know what she said? 'If we took away every kid whose family did drugs, half of the state would be in foster care.'"

"It probably seems that way to her."

Steve frowned at the article, shaking his head. "Richard Taggart, age eighteen. I think *Maine Living* should profile some people like these for a change."

That was the magazine Karen worked for. Its focus was on the idyllic Maine: the lovely old houses, the sailboats and yachts, the island vacation compounds.

Steve looked at the paper again and said, "I'm going to talk to Wendy about this on Monday."

～

But Wendy wasn't in on Monday. She'd had an emergency call to respond to and wouldn't be in all day. Anne wasn't in either.

Steve went to his office and sat at his desk. It was rainy and cool and dark outside. The lilac in the parking lot was already past its prime, its blossoms faded and tinged with brown. They had lasted exactly one week. Their demise made Steve sad—abnormally so. The story about the Taggart boy kept eating at him.

A sound in the hall, a door coming open. Anne. Maybe she'd have the time to go to the Taggarts'. He went to her room.

She stood at her window, looking out.

"Good morning," Steve said.

She turned. She didn't smile, didn't speak. She looked like she'd been crying.

"Anne...?"

She shook her head. "It's just so horrible," she said. "I still can't believe it."

"Anne, what?"

Her lips were quivering. "Jimmy," she said. "That little boy I told you about? The one who went back to his natural mother?"

"Yeah?"

"He's dead."

"Oh Jesus, what happened?"

"She killed him," Anne said. "Stuck his head in the toilet and drowned him."

"My God."

"She was trying to toilet train him."

"Jesus."

"I told them she wasn't ready to take him back, what the hell do you have to do?" Her shoulders heaved. She looked down at her desk. "I don't know, I don't know, he was such an adorable little guy. It's just not fair."

"Oh, Anne."

"I have to go meet with the foster parents. Wendy's already there."

"Wendy's his worker?"

Anne nodded. "I can't really blame her, you can't predict..." Biting her lip and shaking her head, she turned and looked outside again. "I *do* blame her!" she said in a quick burst, "Goddamn it, I *do!*"

Anne left. Steve went back to his office. He thought of the last time he'd gone to the Taggarts', Vernella there in the living room, her eyes alive with rage. He thought of how Mrs. Taggart had struggled with Becca, had dragged her across the rug, had called her a devil. He picked up his briefcase and went down the stairs.

~

When he got there, the front door was open. The dog was not on its chain. The bare earth surrounding its stake was littered with dolls and parts of dolls shiny with rain. The puddle beside the path that led from the door to the mailbox was huge again, and in it a doll's head floated, half submerged.

Steve parked on the side of Stickney Lane with the engine and wipers still going. He wondered why he had bothered to come and considered just driving away. He thought: Why the hell is the door open, damn it? It's *raining*. What's *wrong* with these people?

He looked at the steering wheel, shaking his head. This is stupid, he thought. I don't want to go in there. What the hell would I *do* in there?

When he looked at the house again, there was Vernella. Her bulk filled the doorway. She was barefoot, rain staining her shorts and shirt, the same black shorts and shirt she had worn before.

He saw the knife then, there in her right hand, down by her side, by her rippled and bruised huge thigh. A butcher knife, at least a foot long, and a shock traveled over his shoulders. He reached for the door handle, opened the door part way, then stopped. Vernella just stood there, motionless. Rain fell on Steve's arm, soaked the sleeve of his shirt. His pulse was thick in his neck.

And then in a flash Becca shot through the doorway, barefoot and shirtless, in shorts. Vernella screamed "Devil!" and raised the knife.

Steve threw open his door. Becca saw him and turned, then skidded and fell in the mud. Steve grabbed her around her bare waist with one arm and lifted her up.

She wriggled and kicked, her mouth going open and shut like a fish out of water. He ran with her toward the car. She bit his wrist. He winced and grunted and opened the door on the passenger side, put her onto the seat. Pushed the lock down and slammed the door.

She scrambled across to the driver's side, to the open door, as he ran around the car. He caught her and slid her across the seat. "I'm not going to hurt you," he said. She made a gasping noise, her face pure terror, and beat at him with her fists. "Just stop it," he said, and caught her forearms and held them tight. "Just stop it now, you're going to be all right. I'm not going to hurt you."

She trembled all over. Her eyes were wild. With an odd little moaning sound, she started to cry.

He let her go and she slumped down next to the door with her hands on her face. She wept, her thin chest heaving. Steve looked at the house through his rain spattered glasses, his heart beating quickly. The doorway was empty.

The car was still running. Steve took out his handkerchief, wiped off his glasses, looked at the house again. Still nobody there. "We're just going to go for a little ride," he said, shifting into reverse, "then I'll bring you right home."

Becca cowered against the door as he backed up and turned around. She reached for the door handle, grabbed it and pulled.

"Don't do that," Steve said. "You could fall out, Becca, it's dangerous."

Did she understand? He could see that she didn't know how to work the lock, and thank God for that. She tugged at the handle desperately as he drove up the muddy gravel road; then, defeated, slouched into the seat with her hands on her face and wept again, and then with a wail she said, "Mama!"

The word—the first he had ever heard her utter—sent a thrill through Steve's heart. "We'll go back and see Mama soon," he said, "but first we'll take a ride."

"I want my Mama!"

"Soon," Steve said.

"No! No!"

"Right after our ride."

"*No.*" The word was a moan.

"We won't be long."

She wept again.

Pretty soon they were out on the Brisbane Road. Becca sat with her knees against her chest, her toes curled over the edge of the seat. She covered her eyes with her hands and started shaking. Suddenly Steve felt cold.

He'd planned to go to the police, but now he had second thoughts. He didn't know what they'd make of this. He had no authority, none whatsoever, but Becca's life had been threatened and surely they'd understand. Or would they?

He started to sweat, and his sweat was cold. When Child Protective took a kid they went to a judge, got an order signed. In a really extreme situation they sometimes skipped the order. "But," Wendy had warned, "you better have a cop along, or you could be in trouble."

Becca started to rock back and forth with her eyes still covered, whimpering, softly sobbing. "It's okay, Becca," Steve said, but she paid no attention, just rocked and sobbed. "It's okay, it's going to be fine," he said—and a memory came back.

He must have been just about Becca's age. In the hospital with his mother, waiting, waiting, and finally some people in white came to see him. They lifted him out of the bed, put him up on a high metal table with wheels and started to roll him away. Panic stricken, he cried out, "Mommy!" and one of the people, a woman, said pleasantly, "Everything's going to be fine," and he knew she was saying it nicely like that because it wasn't true. He rolled down the corridor, flat on his back, getting dizzy with everything rushing past, and then with his heart beating wildly, huge in his throat, they pushed him through double doors. Some people dressed all in green were there, strange men with their faces masked so that only their eyes and eyebrows showed. One of them held a black funnel of rubber and said, "Just breathe," as he lowered the funnel over Steve's mouth and nose. Steve cried out, "No!" was caught and held as the dark pressed down—

When he looked at Becca again, he felt sick.

By the time they got out to Route One she had stopped her crying. Her hands were on her forehead now, overlapping, forming a visor. She stared at the floor, still shaking.

Steve didn't know where the local police station was. The State Police were in Taylor, twenty-five miles away. And what if her mother had already called the police? What if they caught him before he could come to them? He let out a breath and said softly, "Christ."

He'd call Child Protective. He'd call and explain what he'd done, describe where he was, ask them how to proceed. He tried to remember what places between here and Taylor might have a phone outside. There wasn't much along this stretch of road: a couple of antique shops, a greenhouse, a hardware store...

But what would he do with Becca while he used the phone? He couldn't just leave her alone in the car, take the chance that she might work the lock and run off, and he certainly couldn't take her with him, the way she was carrying on. *Damn.* A phone call was out of the question, he'd have to go to the cops.

He glanced at her quivering there, hunched up. She was rocking hard, and her lips were pressed tightly together.

"Becca?"

She gave no sign that she'd heard him, just stared straight ahead with her hands on her forehead.

"Do you have to go to the bathroom?"

No answer.

"Do you have to pee?"

Again nothing; then, slowly, she nodded

"Do you have to pee bad, or can you wait?"

She shook her head no.

"You can't wait?"

She shook her head no again.

"Okay," he said.

There was nothing along this stretch of Route One except trees: evergreens, birches and oaks with pale tiny green leaves. He drove onto the shoulder and parked, turned off the engine, got out. The rain was now steady and cold. He inserted the key in the lock on the passenger side and opened the door. "Okay," he said, "you can pee in those trees over there, come on."

She slid off the seat and stood on the roadside gravel. The earth sloped gently upward here. She glanced at him furtively, breathing hard, like an animal in a trap. "Right there in those trees," he said. She turned and scrambled up the slope. She reached the stand of evergreens, ducked under the branches, then started to run.

"Becca!" Steve said—and took off after her.

And what if the cops come now? he thought. *What if the cops come now and catch me here in these woods with her?*

Becca slipped through the trees as slick as a snake, her wet skin shining. Steve was amazed by how fast she could run in bare feet. The branches he struck soaked his shirt, his face. "Becca! Stop!"

She looked at him over her shoulder, her face filled with fear, then tripped on a root and went sprawling. Clawing at leaves, she righted herself, and Steve caught her.

She beat at him savagely, screaming, "I want my Mama! I want my Mama!" She slashed at his eyes, her nails tore his cheek, he flinched—and his glasses went flying.

He instantly let her go and, panicked, knelt on the spongy earth. His glasses had dark plastic rims and were lost in the fallen dead leaves. He cursed under his breath. If his glasses were gone, what then? He wouldn't find Becca. He'd find his way back to the road, he could hear traffic speeding along back there, but he wouldn't be able to drive. He cautiously crawled on his hands and knees, picked up a curving twig by mistake, threw it down. "Damn," he said. Then he found them.

He took out his handkerchief, wiped off the lenses, wiped off his face, put his glasses back on. Shoving his handkerchief into his pocket again, he stood, looked around at the dripping trees. Above the sound of the steady rain he could hear something else: rushing water, a stream, and he thought, *Oh Christ.*

He started to walk toward the sound, heart roaring, bright fear in his chest.

He saw something then at the edge of his vision, quick movement. Perhaps just a bird or a squirrel, but he started to walk that way, toward a huge boulder speckled with lichen.

Then, just for an instant, the side of her face at the edge of the boulder. *Thank God.*

The woods were fairly open here, with spindly balsams and tamaracks. Steve walked slowly through matted wet leaves; passed a couple of beer cans and two plastic bags filled with trash.

He was ten feet away from the rock when she bolted. He ran. The brook was down a small incline, and she slid on the moss and leaves and was into the water. He ran down after her, grabbed her around her waist. She kicked and screamed.

"Becca, stop it, I'm not going to hurt you!" he said. "Come on, now, this is enough!"

She elbowed his stomach. The water was halfway up to his knees. It was brown as tea and was moving swiftly across black stones. He almost slipped, but caught himself. She jammed her elbow into his ribs, again, again, again. He fought his way up the bank and back through the trees, his heart pounding hard in his throat. She bit his arm and he winced. "Goddamn it!"

They reached the car. He lifted her up and she peed: on his leg, on the seat, and she screamed, "I want my Mama! I want my Mama! " He pushed the lock down, closed the door.

He slid behind the wheel out of breath, soaking wet; slammed his door. Becca kicked at him viciously. "Stop it, all right?" he said. "I'm taking you home."

"Right now!" she said, her hands tight fists. "You take me home right now!" The skin around her lips was white.

"Okay!" he said. "I will! Now you behave!"

He started the car. The wipers pushed rhythmically at the rain. He waited for a truck to pass, then made a U-turn.

Becca was quiet and shaking again, hunching against the door. The car smelled strongly of urine. Steve's cheek was starting to sting where she'd scratched him.

Becca was running away from Vernella, Vernella was holding a knife, he wanted to keep Becca safe—that's what he would tell Mrs. Taggart. But would she believe him?

Now Becca was whining again. "Becca, stop it," he said, "we're going home, it's okay now, you don't have to cry anymore."

Her face was contorted, her skinny chest heaved. "I want my Mama!"

"You'll get her. Soon."

On the Brisbane Road the rain suddenly stopped. Steve turned off the wipers and looked at Becca, who shielded her eyes with her hands again. Her left cheek was scratched and so were her arms, and pine needles clung to her slimy bare chest. Her hair was soaked and plastered against her skull.

My God, Steve thought, *what ever possessed me?*

He should have gone straight to the cops by himself. But Jesus, Vernella was holding the knife and Becca was running away and there just wasn't time for that—time to even think straight. And now crazy Vernella would still be there with her knife...

Or maybe the cops would be there instead.

Steve thought about that. Okay. He'd tell them his strategy was to remove the child from danger, hoping her mother would call the police. He'd wait for a while, then drive back hoping to find them there. If they hadn't arrived, he'd go to the station.

And what if the cops *weren't* there right now? Would Mrs. Taggart call them, press charges? Who *knew* what a person like that would do? Jesus Christ, what a fool he had been! One stupid impulsive move could mean the end of everything—his job, adoption...

They went down muddy Stickney Road. A wide splash of sun lit the field, then faded. Becca was crying again.

"We're almost there," Steve said. "It's okay, Becca, you'll see your Mama soon."

Then suddenly, surprisingly, he felt like crying too. *Karen will be shocked,* he thought, *she'll be totally shocked.* "Becca, stop," he said. "Please stop."

When the house appeared, Becca sprang to her knees. "Here we are," Steve said. "You're home again."

No cop car there. Instead, a black pickup in back of the brown sedan, with rusted fenders and a missing bumper.

Steve pulled over and turned off the engine. Becca yanked at the door handle frantically. Steve reached across her, opened the door, and out she flew down the muddy path, past the puddle. She slipped and fell, got up and was running again. The door of the house was still open. She ran inside.

Steve got out of the car. His shoes and pants and shirt were soaked. He looked at the puddle, that doll's head floating, its eyes rolled back, and started to walk down the path. He had to explain to Mrs. Taggart, he couldn't just drive away, she'd press charges for sure. He hoped to God Vernella had left...

He took a deep breath, wiped wet off his forehead, and then from within the house he heard, "Don't kill him, Vernon! Please, Vernon, don't kill him!"—Mrs. Taggart's hysterical voice.

Then a man with a rifle was in the doorway, a very big man with long shaggy gray hair poking out from below a red baseball cap. He wore grease-stained green workpants and black work shoes and a gray T-shirt. The T-shirt was riddled with holes, through which patches of pale hairy stomach protruded. "You stop right there!" the man said loudly. "Just stop right there!" and he lifted the gun to his shoulder.

"Don't kill him!" the cry came again, and now, in the shadows behind the man, Steve could see Mrs. Taggart, could see her pale face and her tufted red hair. He swallowed with effort, weak in his chest; when he spoke, something caught in his throat.

"I was scared she was going to get hurt," he said. "Vernella was holding a knife, Mrs. Taggart, I thought that she might hurt Becca."

"You took my little *girl!*" the huge man roared. His beefy unshaven face was infused with a purplish red.

"I'm sorry," Steve said. "I was scared she'd get hurt, that's all. Could you put the gun down?"

The man fired. The bullet tore into the puddle beside Steve's leg, splashing his slacks, making him jerk, sending a cold jolt of fear through his chest. The doll's head bobbed.

"Mr. Taggart—"

The huge man aimed and fired again. Again the bullet struck the puddle, drenching Steve's leg. "You just shut up!" he yelled. "You leave my family alone! You got no right to tell us how to live, no right at all!"

A quick crisp wind had started up and was tearing the sky apart. Chunks of gray cloud sped away over brilliant blue. A stiff ray of sun hit the roof of the house and was gone, and Steve suddenly felt unreal, as if he were acting, as if he were in a play. *He's just trying to scare me,* he said to himself, but his mind was racing, his heart was racing, a shudder went down his back. He thought: *If I just turn around and walk away, will he actually shoot me?*

A black fly came at his eye and he flinched, but kept himself from swatting it. He couldn't risk movement like that, it could startle Taggart. He squinted as the insect attacked his eyelid. Another one came, and another; dug into his scalp.

This time the bullet struck on Steve's right, sending up mud and stones, and his heart pounded even harder, as hard as it had when the man whose daughter was "going blind" had yelled at him. He pictured Karen, at work, knowing nothing of this.

"You goddamn outstaters come here an' tell us the way to live!" the man said. "Goddamn rich people! Rich sons of bitches!"

"I grew up in Falmouth," Steve said. His voice sounded distant, rang in his ears. "I'm from Maine." He felt a black fly on his lip.

"Don't kill him, Vernon!" wailed Mrs. Taggart. "He's nice, he works for SSI. You used to get SSI."

The huge man fired again, the water flew, and he yelled, "If we was rich you'd never do this shit! This shit don't happen to rich people, nobody takes their kids away!"

Steve stood perfectly still, unreal, the man from TV. He remembered the first time he'd come here, that soap opera up on the packing crate: *This can't be happening!* How easy for that gun to "slip," he thought, for there to be an "accident."

Black flies swarmed at his eyelids, biting; he didn't dare swat them away. Pressing his lips together, he told himself: *Think only of positive things,* and he thought of Karen again but it made him sad. "Karen," he said in a whisper, blinking, the black flies biting, his eyelids itching and swelling. He looked away from the man with the gun, at the mangled apple tree in bloom against the splendid sky. He saw the tire hanging there and thought of the farm, so long ago, then looked at the kitchen window: and there was Becca, up on the table, her forehead and small palms flat on the dirty glass.

The rifle went off again and the puddle erupted, terribly close this time. Steve stared at the kitchen window, at Becca's pale face, then took a deep breath and looked down at the puddle. The doll's head was gone.

A black fly attacked with a high-pitched buzz; burrowed into his ear canal. He looked back at the house.

There was nobody in the doorway now and nobody at the window. He gritted his teeth and slapped his ear, stumbling backward a step. Then he went to his car.

He started the engine, swung around sharply, drove off. The tires slammed into the potholes, jarring his spine.

By the time he reached the Brisbane Road, his eyes were gummy slits. Shivering now and drained of strength, he pressed down hard on the gas. His hands were clammy on the wheel and his hot head throbbed.

He'd been lucky, damn lucky, he told himself. He hadn't

been hit, Becca hadn't been hurt. And maybe he'd have more luck and his eyes wouldn't close all the way from the venom, his throat wouldn't close, he'd be able to breathe, and the Taggarts wouldn't press charges. He thought of what Karen would say when she saw him, and how to explain, and this time he pictured her lying in bed, pale, after her last miscarriage, her cheeks wet from crying. What came to him then was the image of Becca, her face at the window, her hands and forehead pressing against the glass, and he thought of Julia, the daughter who only existed in dreams. *Stop it, stop it!* he said to himself. *Just stop it! You're lucky!*

Lost

Doug tossed a handful of blueberries into his mouth. The girl, observing this from where she squatted in the field, looked at the berries in her palm, then ate a few. Her mother, whose name was Joyce, said in her crisp British accent, "We've tried to teach them to wash their fruit before they eat it, but here I suppose that's hopeless."

"I'm sure these berries won't hurt them," Doug said.

Joyce arched her eyebrows. "I do hope you're right."

Her husband, Edward, said, "Let's try to fill our pails before we gorge ourselves." The children, intent on their picking, seemed not to hear.

A wide path cut through the sloping field, and in it were Doug's wife Lynne, and her friend, Eileen. Eileen said, "Mike?"

Her husband, tall and thin, with curly gray hair and beard. He stood a few yards away from her, inspecting the berries in his hand. Discarding a leaf, he ate them. "What?"

"We're taking a walk to the pond, want to come?"

"I guess so."

Eileen made a visor out of her hand. "Hey Joyce, want to walk to the pond? Edward?"

"Certainly," Edward said.

Doug looked at the black rusted car at the field's east end, near the dark line of trees. He looked at the clothesline that went from a hook on the barn to a pole near the lone apple tree. The line sagged badly. He wondered how long it had been since wash had hung there.

"You coming, Doug?" Lynne's big straw hat cast a shadow across her eyes.

"No, I'll stay here," Doug said. He didn't especially like this English couple, friends of Mike and Eileen.

"Martin and Alice," called Edward, eating a berry, and started to walk toward the path. The children, some forty feet off, stood slowly and came his way.

Lynne pointed east then swept her arm south.

"So how many acres this side of the road?" Mike said.

"A hundred and ten."

"Quite a fine piece of land," Edward said.

"It has two thousand feet on the pond."

"Good gracious," Joyce said.

Everyone walked down the path except Doug, the children lagging behind to pick berries. Soon they were gone in the trees and their voices died, and Doug was alone with the fields and the brilliant sky. From here he couldn't see the pond, but up by the house, at the top of the hill, a slice of it was visible.

He started back up to the house. He'd been here a couple of times before and didn't want to go inside again, it was too depressing: the stained wallpaper and peeling paint, the moldy sofa, the sagging ceilings, the tin of petrified cookies on the cast iron kitchen stove. The photograph of a child, framed, in the dirt on the living room floor.

There had once been a time when houses like this excited him, when his mind had raced with thoughts of how to rearrange the space and open things up and bring in more light. He and Lynne would measure the rooms and spend hours discussing the options, staying up late drawing sketches and plans. Even if they had no serious interest in buying a place, it was something they loved to do, sort of a hobby.

Lynne still loved to do it, and Doug wished that he did too. But now as he looked at the green wooden storm door askew on its hinges, the torn lace curtain behind the glass, the pale little plastic palm tree tacked to the jamb by the broken buzzer; remembered the brown linoleum rug strewn with plaster and rags and old junk mail, the sadness hit him again and he turned away.

He walked to the end of the drive, to the asphalt road. The property lay on both sides of this road, most of it on the east with the house and pond; but a pretty large piece stretched away to the west, about sixty-five acres of woods that bordered a stream—so the realtor said.

Doug walked down the road, looking into the woods. Somewhere there must be a path. A car and a pickup truck went by, stirring the tall yellow grass at the edge of the gravel shoulder.

A sale sign was nailed to a tree up ahead. Doug went to it—and there was the entry into the woods, a one-lane road that hadn't been used in years. The ruts of tires were barely visible, the spine of earth between them thick with grass. The road would surely lead to the stream if he followed it far enough, but how long was the road?

He decided to walk for fifteen minutes. If he didn't find the stream by then, he'd head back.

The land sloped downward gently as he made his way past spruce and fir and birch and maple and pine. At first the road was rocky, with washed-out spots, but soon it turned spongy and soft. It was scattered with broken branches and leaves, and every so often was blocked by a fallen tree.

Behind him, at a distance now, Doug heard a car go by on the sun-baked asphalt. Years ago he had looked at some land by himself, had walked down an old abandoned lane like this, crossed a desolate stretch of dead skeletal trees and had lost his bearings. The sound of traffic had led him back to his starting point. To hear it now was comforting. If he only walked for fifteen minutes, he shouldn't be out of its range.

He reached an open place, a ledge outcrop that was bordered by tall thick blueberry bushes loaded with fruit. Lowbush berries were common, but not the highbush types. These particular berries were shiny and almost black. Suddenly hungry, Doug stripped off a handful and ate them. Their flavor was sweet and subtle.

He looked at a distant bank of clouds and ate more berries. He loved this place: the wide rocky shelf of stone with its gray-green lichen, its stand of laurel, the high sun glorious, striking the mica flecks in the rock, shining like silver on tiny dark blueberry leaves.

He closed his eyes and filled his lungs with the clean Maine air and said to himself: *I'm alive!* He breathed, he breathed, then opened his eyes and stripped more berries from the bush. Ate slowly, savoring the juices as he started to walk again.

The road grew narrow, became a path. No car or pickup had ever come down this far. A cloud hid the sun and the trees went dark.

Doug looked at his watch. Fifteen minutes had already passed, but the time he had spent on the ledge didn't count. He would walk for another five minutes or so, then go back. He was wearing a shortsleeve shirt and now a mosquito had found his elbow. He smacked it dead, flicked it away.

He came to another ledge, a smaller one, only twenty-five feet or so wide. Ahead, the woods were dense. Turning around, he made note of an old white birch by the side of the path, then went to the rim of the ledge and stared at the trees.

The path had ended. That didn't seem right. Surely it wouldn't end till it came to the stream, he just couldn't spot it, and surely the stream couldn't be far off. He listened, but heard no sound of water. Maybe the stream was too small to be heard unless you were right on top of it.

Now he could hear the drone of a small plane, and looked at the sky. The clouds had moved in rapidly, and the plane was hidden. He checked his watch again: it was time to go. The others would be back from their walk to the pond and would wonder about him.

He turned around and looked for the large white birch—and saw five of them. How could that be? Why hadn't he noticed those others before? He went to the nearest one, but found no path. He went to the others. No path.

Impossible. It had to be next to one of these trees, but he went to each of the birches again and still couldn't find it. He looked at the sky. It was covered with clouds; no sun at all.

He thought he was facing east, but wasn't sure. He listened for traffic, but all he could hear was the plane.

He walked: through fallen limbs and rocky outcrops, skirting thick stands of brush. The land sloped upward, making him fairly sure he was headed right.

But suppose he was slightly off—even only a few degrees? It could make a huge difference. A few degrees could mean a walk of miles in the wrong direction.

He came to a little gully, crossed it, climbed up the other side. His heart was beating quickly now, and his right hip hurt: the arthritis from where they had drilled the holes in his bones. And what if it got so bad that he couldn't walk, or the cramps came on, or he stumbled and twisted his ankle?

He stopped for a moment. His heart was beating, beating, beating, and now he was sweating hard. His head was filled with the beat of his heart and the hum of the plane, still directly above. He smacked at another mosquito.

His heart did not slow, but he started to walk again, fighting his way through brush and up a steep hill. Now he had no idea where he was. For all he knew, he might be heading back to where those birches were. For God's sake, he'd done it again, he was lost! What a fool!

If he didn't reach the road in another ten minutes, he'd start calling out for help—if the plane was gone. If it wasn't gone, they'd never hear him. If it was, he might hear the traffic again and wouldn't need to call.

But what if the plane went away and he didn't hear any traffic? What if it went away and he called and they didn't hear him?

They'd search for him. And suppose he passed out and didn't hear *them?* The police would use dogs and eventually find him...

But maybe not. On Valentine's Day last year an elderly man in western Maine went out for a walk and never came back. A fruitless search by cops and family and friends had lasted for several days. It wasn't till nine months later that "tippers"—people gathering evergreen boughs for wreaths—had come across his corpse.

What a mess, Doug said to himself as he pushed aside branches that blocked his way. *What a stupid mess. Just take a little tour of the woods and not tell anyone where you're going. Forty-seven years old, and that's how smart—*

A sudden astounding pain in his calf and he cried out and fell to his knees. Gritting his teeth, he kneaded the rigid muscle. The chemo had damaged his nervous system, causing these horrible cramps. He worked on the muscle until it relaxed, then got to his feet again. He moved off slowly now to avoid more cramps, but his heart didn't slow at all.

Another hill. At its crest was a ledge. The one he had stopped at before, with the highbush berries?

No, nothing but lowbush berries here. He sat on the rock out of breath with his arms on his knees, and his heart beat so fast and so hard that he thought it would burst.

And would that be so bad? he asked himself. To die right now, right here, in this beautiful place? For his heart to give out in a bright blaze of pain, would that be so bad? The best of his life was surely behind him and God only knew what lay ahead. The disease could come back at any time and chances were good that it *would* come back, and that meant a painful, lingering death—or a bone marrow transplant, which, if things didn't go exactly right, could also mean death. Huge doses of chemo, fevers, infections, then death or impairment: of kidneys, liver, heart, lungs, eyes, ears, brain.

In the depths of the chemo he'd gone through before, the black winter nights of retching that tore his stomach and throat for hours to finally end in cold weak shaking, he sometimes asked himself if he wanted to live. The answer had always been yes.

And he wanted to live now, too.

He fought for breath as his heart beat on, skin slick with sweat. He held his head and stared at the stone at his feet, the flecks of black and gold. The hip where they drilled for a sample of bone marrow every three months was throbbing hard.

He kept holding his head. And the sound of the plane was softer, fading, and now—the growl of a truck: louder and louder, and then it was gone. He was heading the right way after all.

He timed his heart. Another six minutes went by before it was beating calmly.

He stood, took a long deep breath and walked through a field of lowbush berries. There, up ahead on the left, a utility pole.

He met the road about fifty feet north of the spot where he'd entered the woods. When he got to the house, Lynne was walking around in the field in front of the place. The English children were helping their mother pick berries. The sky was a flat, bright gray.

Doug's hip was aching and so were his shoulders and legs. He squatted and picked a few berries, then went to Lynne. "So what did they think of the pond?" he asked.

"Eileen just loved it, loves the entire property, but Mike's not interested."

"How come?"

"The house is too much work."

"It *is* a lot of work."

"We fixed worse places."

"Yes, we did," Doug said. "We did all kinds of things."

Lynne frowned and said, "How'd you scratch yourself up like that?"

Doug looked at his arm. It was bleeding above the spot where they'd put in the chemo lines. He said, "I was walking around in the woods across the road."

"What's it like over there?"

"It's beautiful. Kind of buggy."

He looked across the sloping field to the rusted car, the line of trees. Above the trees, a silver loop: the pond's east rim. He looked at the empty clothesline attached to the barn. In the distance, the drone of a plane.

"On Friday I go for my tests," he said.

Adjusting her hat, Lynne frowned again. "You didn't think I'd forget that, did you?"

"Of course not."

"Then why did you mention it now?"

"It's just been on my mind."

The Tip

On the Mass Pike the nozzle had leaked and gas had run over Gene's palm. That was hours ago, but whenever he brought his hand to his face—to adjust his glasses, to rub his chin—there was the smell.

The tank was low again. A sign for a service plaza appeared in the mist and Gene said, "We'll stop at this place."

"And you'll let *them* pump it," Suzanne said.

"I don't have any choice," Gene said, "it's not self-serve on this highway."

Connecticut flurries had turned to a thin cold drizzle in Jersey, and here in Maryland the drizzle was mixed with fog. It had been a long drive; Gene's neck was stiff and his shoulders hurt. Another two hours should do it, though. He pictured himself in his parents' apartment, holding a whiskey and water.

"The turnoff's right here, don't miss it," Suzanne said.

"I'm not going to miss it," Gene said.

Four rows of pumps stood under a high flat roof. There were cars at all but one of them, and Gene pulled the Honda up to it.

They waited, but nobody came. An attendant was servicing somebody two rows away. Gene saw a couple of guys in the glass payment booth; they were laughing and joking around. "Let's go somewhere else," he said.

"Don't be so impatient," Suzanne said, "we're really low. You get back on the road and we start *that* thing."

"I'm sure I can make it—"

"Here he comes."

He was thirty or so, tall, with thick dark hair and high cheek-bones. Above his jacket pocket, upper left, red script said "Wayne."

Gene rolled the window down and a stream of mist entered the car.

"Can't reach," the attendant said. "You have to turn around."

Gene's jaw was tight as he started the engine. "Why the hell don't they get longer hoses?" he said, pulling forward. "Or why don't the people who make these cars put all gas tanks on the driver's side?" He turned near an overstuffed trash can and came back up to the pump. The guy was now servicing somebody else.

They waited, nose to nose with a yellow Saab that had just pulled in. "And now I'll have to back up to get out," Gene said, "unless her Saab has its tank on the wrong side too and he makes *her* move."

The attendant appeared again, next to Suzanne, who cracked her window. "Fill it with regular, please," she said.

The guy took the gas cap off, stuck the hose in the tank, then went to the Saab.

The whir of the pump, and Suzanne said, "We really should go see Carol."

"If she calls," Gene said.

"I think we should see her anyway, it's been three years."

"We're not going to spend forever down here."

"What will it take, a couple of hours?"

"Half a day. Oh, Christ."

"What."

"The pump clicked off. Where the hell's that guy?"

They couldn't see him anywhere. "He *has* to come back soon," Suzanne said.

Gene shook his head. "They've got you," he said. "They don't give a damn about service, where else can you go? Five miles off the highway and pump it yourself in the rain? With another goddamn broken nozzle, probably? He knows he'll never see you again, so why should he care?"

"Here he is."

The guy pressed the lever and held it. Gene saw the dark blue jacket, its sleeve, its back, through the smeary window. He looked at the numbers turn on the pump in the gray wet light and took out his wallet. "Sixteen? I can't tell."

"I can't really see it either," Suzanne said. "I *think* it's sixteen."

The sound of the nozzle scraping the fill pipe, the sound of the gas cap being turned. The attendant coming around to Gene's side of the car. Gene rolled down the window and gave him the money.

The guy raised his eyebrows. He nodded and said, "Oh," and walked away. He went to the Saab again.

Gene started the engine. "Weird, he must be on drugs."

The wipers erased the drizzle as Gene backed up. As the car passed the pump, Suzanne said, "Fifteen. It was only fifteen."

"What?" Gene said, his voice rising. "I thought you said sixteen."

"*You* said it was sixteen."

"And you agreed."

"We saw it wrong."

Gene gritted his teeth. "I gave the guy an extra buck, and he didn't say a word."

"He's over there, you can still get it back."

"Goddamn it," Gene said.

"Well, go get it back."

"Yeah, right, in this chaos?" Another car stood at the pump they'd just left. A different attendant lifted the hose, flipped the lever.

"Forget it," Gene said.

"If you feel that strongly about it—"

"I don't," Gene said.

He drove up the access lane to the highway. "The creep knew I gave him too much and he just walked off. The *bastard*."

Suzanne shook her head.

~

"Bad day," Cindy said.

Wayne looked at his franks and beans. He was quiet a moment, then said, "Something happened today that...oh hell, I don't know."

"What?"

"This guy." Wayne was still looking down at his plate. "That goddamn Hastings was giving me grief, and I was ripped, so I wait on this guy and tell him the hose won't reach. It could reach. I was pissed at Hastings, and take it out on this guy. I just wanted to make him move. So he does, I can tell he's steamed, and I take my time. The nozzle clicks off when he's halfway full, and he's waiting. I let him wait. I know he's steamed when I top him off, but before I can even tell him how much it is, he pays me—and gives me an extra buck. He gives me a *tip*. I was so surprised, I didn't even say thanks. I said 'Oh,' and I walked away. 'Oh,' that's what I said, like a dork. It bothered me all afternoon, it still bothers me now. It's Christmastime, right? Everybody's like out of their minds, and what do I do, I treat this guy like dirt and he gives me a tip. I can't get over it."

Cindy was frowning and chewing her lip. "Well, nothing you can do about it now."

"But there is," Wayne said. "There is, I can quit treating people like dirt when I'm in a bad mood."

Cindy stayed silent.

"That's right," Wayne said. "Well, maybe I'm wrong, he was being sarcastic or something, but...nah, it's *Christmas*, he gave me a *tip*. Goddamn it, I'm not gonna do that shit anymore. I'm not. I mean it."

"You want me to warm up your food?" Cindy said.

"I'm not hungry," Wayne said. He pushed at his beans with his fork and frowned. "Maine tags. You ever been there?"

"No."

"Me neither. Christ, I didn't even say thanks. What a dork."

~

In the dark, Suzanne said, "Come on, let it go."

Beside her in the study's hide-a-bed, Gene said, "I should've just pulled away when he said the hose wouldn't reach."

"And go where? We were really low."

"I could've found another place."

"Off the highway, you mean?"

"That's right."

"It wasn't worth the trouble. Let it go."

Gene stared up at the ceiling, his wrist on his forehead. "It's just so *typical* of me to be passive about it. I should've gone up to the guy and demanded the dollar back."

Suzanne exhaled. "Let's get some sleep."

Gene could still smell the gas on his hand, just faintly. He saw the attendant again.

"I've learned," he said. "Next time I'll get the money back, I'm not going to let these creeps get away with this stuff."

"All this turmoil over a dollar," Suzanne said.

"It's not just over a dollar," Gene said, "it's over a lot more than that. I'm telling you, this is the last time they get away with it. I've learned."

She touched his shoulder. "How's your neck?"

"The whiskey helped."

"Good, let's just get some sleep."

Ride

Paul couldn't remember the last time he'd stood on this downtown corner to wait for the bus. He thought of a time with his mother here ages ago, in his childhood, holding her hand, eyes blurred from the doctor's drops; a time in college, after a basketball game, the snow swirling down in white sheets; a sweltering day in August after he'd left the cool of department stores, the asphalt throwing up withering waves of heat. Had that been the last time, that hot muggy day? Maybe so.

After his marriage he'd bought a car and stopped using public transit. Once, when it snowed on Christmas day, he and Janice had taken the train to his parents' house, but they never rode the bus.

Today, since Janice was using the car to visit a friend who was ill, Paul had come into town on the train. He'd planned to return the same way, but when he went back to the terminal, he found he had just missed a train and the next one wasn't scheduled to leave for almost an hour. He decided to walk to the bus stop, a block away.

He looked across the street at City Hall, where, thirteen years ago, he and Janice had gotten married. An overcast day in January, not very cold, but raw, and they'd shivered, hand in hand, crossing the courtyard. Today was absolutely beautiful, as good as Philadelphia got: sunny and clear, in the sixties, with just a slight breeze. At this time of year, October, even the downtown air seemed clean.

The bus came up and wheezed to a stop, and Paul and the others, a half dozen black high school students, got on. Paul dropped his fare in the box at the top of the steps. It seemed incredible for a bus to cost so much. When he was a kid, the fare had been twenty cents.

The high school students went straight down the aisle and sat on the long back seat. The front of the bus was full, so Paul also went to the back. There was only one space, on a seat that ran parallel to the sides of the bus.

The seat had a six inch gash in its dark brown fabric, and cream-colored foam stuck out. Paul sat with his shopping bag on his lap so it wouldn't block the aisle. His hips were wedged between two older women, both of whom were black, and he noticed now that he was one of the only whites on the bus. After a year in Maine it was strange to see so many black faces.

Across the aisle, facing Paul, an elderly white man, his shoes scuffed and falling apart, his jacket soiled, a stubble of beard on his chin, stared blankly with rheumy red eyes. On the short seat in front of the long last seat, where the high school kids sat, a young white woman with full round cheeks and raggedly cropped black hair turned her face to the window. Beside her, a young black man in a sportscoat and turtleneck, hands on his knees.

A pair of black women sat next to the shabby white man across the way: a tall one in heels and a dark green dress and a short one wearing flat shoes and a jacket and skirt. Both had handbags and packages on their laps. The tall one was telling the short one about a coat she'd seen that wasn't quite right, and the short one told her to try a store named Golden's.

The bus made its way up the Parkway, into the section where Paul used to live. His old house wasn't visible, but even so, he felt a quick pang in his chest. He'd loved his house and this neighborhood, but city life was impossible now: the real estate taxes were out of sight, the air was so dirty it made his kids cough in their sleep, a man had followed Janice home from the park one day, then called her at night with indecent proposals. Someone had kicked their car window in to get at a bag of plaster they'd left on the seat.

The bus passed the library, came to a stop. A woman got off and no one got on. At the art museum it stopped again. A sign advertised a Chagall exhibit. No museums like this in Maine; the closest one was in Boston, a four hour ride from where Paul lived.

The driver was ready to pull away when a sudden loud popping noise came from outside. The driver, a tall black man with a thin moustache, stood up and whirled sharply, standing on tiptoe and craning his neck. Then more loud sounds, more people stood up, and Paul's startled thought was, *That noise is a gun!* and the tall woman dressed in green screamed and started to run, then tripped and fell to the floor. More screams and more people were falling, on top of the woman in green, and Paul didn't move, just kept sitting there holding his bag, thinking, *This might be it!* In his mind he saw Janice and Peter and Amy, safe in his parent's house. One of the high school girls, her eyes wide and terrified, shouted, "Get out my *way!*" There was banging against the side of the bus and the woman in green yelled, "Get off me! Get off me!" The bus driver said, "It's all right, it's okay now, get up, it's all right," and the people began to untangle themselves and look through the windows, and one of the high school boys said, "Cops," and people went back to their seats again.

"It was chains," a boy in the back seat said.

"You thought it was guns," another kid said. "You jump up, you thought it was guns."

They were laughing, relieved. "You scared to death."

"Yeah, what about you, you runnin' right outta here."

"Yeah—"

The woman in green stood alone in the aisle, and one of her stockings was torn at the knee. "I hurt my leg!" she said in a loud indignant voice. "I tore my stocking and hurt my leg! I'll sue!"

The driver, still standing and facing the back of the bus, said, "You're hurt, we go to the hospital."

"I don't want no hospital."

"You're hurt, that's where we're goin.'"

"I'm not hurt bad enough for that."

"You're hurt bad enough to sue."

"I'm not hurt bad."

"You don't want to go?"

"No."

"I'm willing to take you."

"I don't want to go."

The woman in green sat down again and so did the driver. "I coulda been killed!" the woman said loudly. The driver looked into his mirror, and Paul saw his eyes. "All those people on top of me! Look at my knee! And my bag and my package got smashed!"

The bus pulled away and the white woman next to the window peered out and the kids in the back did too, and the sad-looking white man twisted his neck and looked over his shoulder. "Juss a dumb gang fight," said one of the high school girls.

Paul could see nothing from where he sat: no cops, no kids with chains. He sat there holding his bag and broke out in cold sweat.

"White kids," said the woman in green. "All you hear on the news is black kids fight. If they was black, those cops woulda shot 'em up."

"They were hittin' the side of the bus with chains, I thought it was guns at first," said the young white woman. Her voice was nasal and whiny. The black man beside her, the one in the sportscoat and turtleneck shirt, just stared at his knees. The kids in the back were still laughing and joking around.

"They was black, they be dead," said the woman in green, and the shabby white man muttered something.

She looked at him hard. "You don't think so? Hell yeah, white cops? They be dead."

"Thass right," said a boy in the back seat. "Thass how it is."

"They *deserve* to be shot, no matter *what* color they are," the shabby man said.

"But they won't be less they be black," said one of the high school girls.

The bus made a stop and two people got on: an old black man with a lump on his neck and a young black man in an army jacket and black beret, who was working a toothpick around in his mouth. He walked past Paul and sat with the high school kids. He slapped some hands.

"Hey Fly, when you get out?" asked one of the boys.

"Two days ago," said the guy in the black beret.

"Hey whatchoo in for, anyway?"

"Salt wiff daily weapon."

"No shit, man."

The bus pulled away and the woman in green said, "The white kids, they treat 'em so nice, but if they was black, there be blood on the street right now."

The shabby white man shook his head. "They didn't treat 'em nice."

"What the fuck do you know, old man?" said the guy in the black beret. "You don't know shit!"

The young white woman, scowling, turned her head. "Don't use that kinda language on the bus."

"You shut the fuck up, motherfucker!"

"I will not!"

"You say they treat 'em the same, black or white," said the woman in green. "Is that what you say?"

"The cops took 'em away," the white woman said. "What you want 'em to do, shoot 'em dead?"

"They black they *be* dead," said the woman in green.

"Thass right," said the guy in the black beret. "This country needs a revolution, thass what we're sayin' to *you!*"

The high school kids broke in with, "Yeah, revolution, man!" "We talkin' Malcolm here!"

The shabbily dressed old man mumbled, "Malcolm."

"Yeah, whatta you know?" said the guy in the black beret. "You don't know shit about nothin', old man, juss keep your dumb mouth shut."

"I'll open my mouth as much as I want."

"I'll knock your rotten teeth out!"

The guy in the black beret was standing now, his chest thrust forward, his fist in the air. The kid beside him reached up and grabbed the back of his army jacket. "Hey now Fly, come on."

"I ain't gonna take that shit from him."

"Juss black kids gang fight," the woman in green said. "Thass what the papers an' TV tell us."

"I seen white gang fights on *my* TV," the white woman said.

"Thass bullshit!" the guy in the black beret said.

"I'm a liar?" the white woman said. "Is that what you're sayin'?"

"Thass right! You a lyin' azz*hole!*

Paul suddenly pictured Maine, saw himself on the pond in the rowboat, drifting: the fir-covered hills and the deep blue sky and the crisp slow clouds and no people, no people at all. He thought of getting off at the next stop and catching a different bus. But what if he got off here in this black neighborhood and the guy with the black beret and a bunch of the others decided to get off too and start something with him?

The bus stopped again and two of the high school kids got off, a girl and a boy, and three people got on. When the bus started up, the white woman said, "I think it's crazy. What are we arguing for? I don't like gangs, no matter what color they are."

Paul thought: *For God's sake, just shut up!*

"You fool," the guy in the black beret said. "You dumb white fool."

"Don't call her that," the shabby man said.

"You shut your fuckin' mouth, old man! I'm warnin' you!"

"This what we got to listen to," the woman in green said. "Ignorant fools."

"Yeah?" the white woman said. "You think you're a genius or somethin'? Is that what you think?"

Again the the bus stopped, and this time the guy in the black beret strode down the aisle, shaking his fist. "Revolution, old man," he said as he reached the door. "Motherfuckers like you gone *die!*"

He got off with the rest of the high school boys. Now only a couple of girls remained in the long back seat. The bus moved away past an empty lot with the shell of a burned-out car deep in weeds, past brick walls with obscene graffiti. The shabby man sniffed. "We'll see about that. We'll see who's gonna die."

"Oh shut up!" said the woman in green.

"*You* shut up."

"Goddamn crazy old man."

No more talk after that: the sound of the motor, and everyone sitting in silence. The bus made more stops and more people got off, and soon the two high school girls were gone, and two stops later the woman in green got off with her friend. Three stops after that the white woman got off. As she went down the steps she said, "He called me a motherfucker. *Me*. Does that make sense?" The young black man in the sportscoat slid across the seat to where she'd been sitting and looked out the window.

The shabby man opposite Paul had the seat to himself now. "What did I say?" he asked as he stared at his ruined shoes. "I didn't say nothin' against the guy." He looked at the young black man in the sportscoat. "What did I say?"

The man in the sportscoat kept looking outside. "You juss don't understand niggers," he said. "They so uptight."

The man in the sportscoat left two stops later, and five minutes after that, the shabby old man got off. Soon the bus was half empty and most of the riders were white. Only Paul and the driver were left from the start of Paul's ride.

∽

Paul entered his parents' kitchen, holding his shopping bag. Janice said, "Just in time, the kids are setting the table. How was your trip?"

"I'll tell you at dinner."

"How was the train?"

"Okay, but I took the bus home."

"The bus?" his mother said at the stove. "Nobody takes the bus anymore, it's too dangerous."

"Really."

"*I'd* never take it." She pulled the lasagna out of the oven and set it on top of the stove.

"That looks wonderful, Mom," Paul said. Then to Janice: "So how was your day?"

"We got caught in some traffic on City Line, but other than that it was fine. Judy's doing real well. Just one more chemo and she's done."

"That's great."

Amy came in and said, "Daddy, it's dinner time, you're almost late."

"I know," Paul said. "Come here."

He knelt and put his bag on the floor and gave her a big bear hug. It felt so good, so terribly good. He pictured himself on the bus.

"Daddy, when are we going home to Maine?"

"Tomorrow."

"You're not going to stay through the weekend?" his mother said.

"No, I'd like to head back tomorrow."

"But why?" Janice said.

"I'll tell you at dinner," Paul said.

A Clock in San Diego

They left the party early because of the storm. The snow had started as lazy, dime-sized flakes, then quickly thickened and speeded up until now it came straight at their eyes. The road's dividing line and shoulders were lost in white, and Jeff held the steering wheel hard. Melanie, rigid against the seat beside him, said, "It's good we started out when we did."

"Half an hour to get back home from the Martins'," Jeff said. "It's crazy."

"No, it's just Maine."

"Three inches in less than an hour."

"It's a beauty, all right."

A street lamp materialized on their left. "Here's Lindsey," Jeff said.

"Thank God."

Jeff cautiously eased the Saab around the turn and Melanie said, "There's somebody off the road over there."

Somebody off the road. That was Maine too. Jeff hated to stop, but he gently applied the brakes, pulled over, put the blinkers on. "Okay," he said, "let's see what we've got."

In the ten years he'd lived in Maine, he'd gone off the road three times. Melanie had gone off once. The longest either of them had stayed there had been ten minutes. A trooper had towed Melanie out. Jeff had twice been freed by passing pickup trucks, and the other time, a guy who must have been seventy-five had stopped to help him shovel.

Snow swirled in thick sheets, obscuring the streetlamp's globe. The car—a big old Ford, half tan, half brown—sat at the edge of the halo of light, its trunk tipped toward the woods.

As Jeff and Melanie approached, its engine roared, its rear wheels whined.

Jeff came up to the open window. The engine quieted down, and a young man turned and stared. His face was deeply tanned, but looked unhealthy in the blue lamplight. A shock of thick blond hair flopped over his eyebrows.

"Looks like you need some help," Jeff said.

The young man frowned at his hands on the steering wheel. He pushed the hair back from his eyes and laughed without humor and said, "I need some help." A sixpack with only one bottle remaining sat next to him on the seat.

"We'll give you a push," Jeff said. "Okay?"

The guy nodded. "Okay."

They went to the back of the car and braced themselves against the trunk. The cold bit through their gloves. "We shouldn't be doing this," Melanie said. "He's in no shape to drive."

This was the week's third storm. The snow on the side of the road was two feet deep and the car was in over its hubcaps. "It looks pretty hopeless anyway," Jeff said.

They waited for the motor to race again, but nothing happened. Then the driver's door came open and the man got out. He wore a sweater that was tight and short, and a green and white checkered wool vest. His shoes were loafers. He had no hat or gloves. He stood there, not closing the door, then started toward them with wide-based, faltering steps. "Hey, no," he said. "She gets in and *we* push."

Jeff looked at Melanie. "Okay?"

"Sure." She went to the front of the car.

"Just keep the goddamn wheels straight," the young man said.

"I'll try."

Melanie sat in the driver's seat and closed the door. The young man spread his tanned bare hands on the freezing trunk and yelled, "Okay!"

The wheels began to spin. Jeff pushed. The young man

slipped and fell flat on his face. Jeff helped him up. "I'm okay," the man said. "Hell yes, we're tough." He leaned on the trunk again. The car rocked gently back and forth as Melanie touched the gas, let up, pressed down, let up. The young man mumbled, "Damn!" then shouted, "Keep the wheels straight!" The tires spun. The man yelled, "Whoa!"

The engine idled, gurgled deeply. Staring at the snow, at the spot where he'd fallen, the man said, "She's buried."

"I don't have a shovel," Jeff said. His ears were stinging. It was cold, damn cold.

"She's buried," the young man repeated.

Melanie got out. "No good?" she said.

The man kept staring at the snow. It was streaked with black from the car's exhaust. "No good. She's buried," he said.

"Where do you live?" Jeff asked. He hoped to God it was close.

"Up Lindsey," the man said, his head jerking back.

"So do we," Jeff said. "We'll give you a ride."

The man said, "I'll walk." Snow covered his thick blond hair.

"Are you sure you want to do that?" Melanie said. "It's really cold."

"It really is," the young man said with another laugh. He held his arms out, both palms up, and let snow collect in his hands. "I ain't been cold for seven years, and you know, it feels pretty good—as long as it's temporary."

"You don't have any coat," Melanie said. "Come on, we'll give you a lift."

The man started forward, stopped, staggered backward a step. He looked at Melanie, said, "Okay," and went to the front of his car. He opened the door, grabbed the bottle of beer, rolled the window up, slammed the door. "Okay."

The three of them crossed the road. The man fell into the back of the Saab and yanked the door shut hard.

The car moved softly through the snow, its tires silent, its engine dull. Nobody spoke.

The man got the cap off the beer, took a swig. Leaning forward between the bucket seats, he said, "Where you live?" When he belched, the beer smell was strong.

"In the Nelson house," Jeff said.

The man drank again and said, "The Nelson house. That's on the water. I used to clam down there." He narrowed his eyes. "Do I know you?"

"No," Melanie said. "I'm Melanie Reed, and this is Jeff."

"Reed. I know Weeds, but I don't know Reeds." His grin was unpleasant, almost a sneer. "Billy Lawlor," he said. "I was the all-American boy around here, and know what? I couldn't wait to leave. The navy was my ticket out. I couldn't wait. I still hold the high school record for the four hundred meter run. Fifty point six. That ain't too shabby for a high school kid."

Jeff stared through the windshield. The snow was falling even faster now. "So where do you live?" he said.

"San Diego."

"No, I mean here," Jeff said.

The man drank more beer. "Past Walkers'," he said. He grinned again and said, "Hurt my knee. Three operations on it. Can't run worth a damn anymore."

"That's too bad," Melanie said.

Jeff frowned at the snow, his hands tight on the wheel. He saw the young man's eyes in the rearview mirror. He gingerly touched the brake and said, "Near here?"

"Nah, this is Harris country. I said up past Walkers'. You don't know where Walkers' is? How long you been livin' here?"

"Ten years," Jeff said.

"Ten years, and you don't know where Walkers' is?"

"You tell me when," Jeff said.

The young man said, "I'll tell you when." He flopped back in the seat and said, "Where you from?"

"New Jersey," Melanie said.

"New Jersey." A short, quick laugh. "Too goddamn many niggers and spics down there. I guess that's why you moved."

Dead quiet in the car. The man said, "Is that why you moved?"

"Not really," Jeff said. He was passing his own house now and thought, *Jesus Christ.* The man said, "Too many wetbacks out where I live. Too many friggin' Messicans. I live in San Diego, California. Oh. I told you that. You ever been there?"

"No," Melanie said.

"It's great," the young man said. "Seventy-eight degrees every day, you don't gotta split no wood. None of this kinda shit." He swept his arm toward the window, dark with snow, and muttered, "The goddamn stove."

Melanie looked at Jeff. The young man belched again. "Nelson's got great blueberries," he said. "You ever make blueberry pies?"

"I make as many as I can," Melanie said.

"You do," the man said. "You think you make better pies than my mother does?"

"I really wouldn't know."

The young man sniffed. "You bet your ass you don't. My mother makes the best damn pies around. She makes blueberry, apple, strawberry rhubarb...You don't put cinnamon in yours, I guess."

"You must get off in here somewhere," Jeff said.

"I get off at the Lawlor place, it hasn't moved."

"Hey, come on," Jeff said.

"But they might have to sell it," the young man said. "Taxes too high. Outtastaters come in and buy all the frontage, goddamn taxes shoot through the roof. I used to clam at Nelson's. You clam there?"

"Sometimes."

"No, I mean *clam* there. I don't mean sometimes, I mean *clam.*"

Jeff stared through the windshield; the Saab was just crawling along. They had almost reached the end of the road.

The man said, "San Diego they got lobsters too, but they're different. Know what else they got?"

Dead quiet. Jeff strained to see through the snow.

"A clock on the sidewalk made out of glass and brass. You can see all the gears inside. It's just standin' there right on the sidewalk, all year 'round. Seventy-goddamn eight degrees. Imagine that."

"This has to be your house," Jeff said, and stopped the car.

"I was talkin' about the clock," the man said.

"It sounds marvelous," Jeff said. "Is this your house or not?"

The man squinted. "Yeah, this is it." Leaning back in his seat, he just sat there a minute, and then he propelled himself forward and opened the door. He swigged from his bottle and stumbled out into the snow. "You don't even know the Lawlors? They live on your road."

"Could you shut the door, please?" Jeff said.

The young man swayed a little. "You don't know the Lawlors," he said. "You come here from goddamn New Jersey and live on my road and you don't know shit. I learned about boats on this water, more that I ever learned in the goddamn navy. When I was twelve I had fifty-five traps. That's not too shabby for a twelve year old kid."

"Would you shut the door?"

"You never had traps," the young man said. "You never went swimmin' and slidin' here. You don't even clam. You don't use cinnamon in your pies."

Melanie reached behind her, but couldn't grab the door.

The man's voice rose. He said, "You live here, but didn't earn it! You come here and raise the goddamn taxes and won't let the real Maine people clam and hunt!"

"We gave you a ride," Melanie said. "We went out of our way for you. You ought to be grateful."

"Right," the man said, "I oughta be grateful. Grateful to goddamn summer people."

Jeff knelt on his seat and turned around, stretched out, caught the handle of the open back door.

"You have to be born in Maine and grow up in Maine to know what—"

The slam of the door chopped the sentence off. Jeff backed the car up, shifted into first.

"He's down again," Melanie said.

"I doubt if he felt it," Jeff said.

"Maybe he knocked himself out."

"Then he'll freeze," Jeff said. He drove forward a couple of yards, then stopped and turned the engine off. "Okay," he said. "Okay."

They got out of the car. The headlights died into the snow. Jeff grabbed the young man under the arms and Melanie took his feet. The bottle fell out of his hand. They carried him up to the house, where a round purple light shone over the kitchen door.

Nobody answered their knock, so they went inside and set the man down on the floor. Jeff turned on the lamp above the sink. The man didn't move. Jeff checked the fire in the cast iron stove. It was very low, so he added three sticks of the wood that sat in the bucket beside the brick hearth. On the wall near the stove hung a photograph of the man, years younger, in a cap and gown. Next to that was a photo of a gray-haired woman.

"It's Edna," Melanie said.

"Who?"

"Edna. The woman who sells us rhubarb and asparagus. I knew I recognized that car."

"Christ," Jeff said.

"She gave us those raspberry plants, remember?"

"Of course I remember."

The young man rolled onto his side. He groaned. Snow beat on the window beside the door, sounding like sand. "Come on," Jeff said, "let's get the hell home."

As they drove, he thought about Edna's raspberry plants. All six of them had thrived, and last summer they'd borne a huge crop. He thought of Edna's kitchen again, the photos on the wall. "Maybe we should jack a few deer while we're out here," he said. "Maybe we should go down the beach and smash beer bottles on the rocks. Or break into a few of the summer cottages and steal their TV sets."

"Forget him," Melanie said. "He was just a pathetic drunk."

But Jeff couldn't forget him. In bed he felt cold. Snow ticked against the window panes, and it took him a long time to fall asleep. When he did, he dreamed of a warm bright city he'd never seen and a sidewalk clock of glass and brass, huge snowflakes landing on its face, evaporating with a hiss.

One Day in the Short Happy Life
of Anna Banana

Anna Banana is up with the sun. She checks her watch: five o'clock. Every day she gets up at the same time, five o'clock. She looks at the skylight. The sky is a dense, bright blue. Another nice day. That makes four in a row. Or is it five?

It gets bright so early here, she thinks. In the city it never got bright this early. Or maybe it's just the skylight. She gets out of bed and goes to the bathroom and gets back in bed again. She stares at the ceiling. Through the skylight she sees the tree branches with every leaf perfectly still.

≈

Now the children are up. She can hear them thumping around upstairs. She can hear the little one yelling. What a bugger he is! Soon the children will come down and eat and go off to school and Lois will go to work, then Anna Banana will get up and eat. She is starving now. Why can't she sleep late anymore, at least until seven o'clock? She lies there and stares at the ceiling and her stomach growls.

≈

Anna Banana's son-in-law says, "Oops," as he almost bumps into her. "I'm always in the way," she says. "It's okay," he says. He is on his way upstairs to plaster the walls. Anna Banana's son-in-law stays home and her daughter works. It seems funny to have a man stay home all day; it isn't right. Lois teaches and David stays home and fixes the house and cooks and does the wash. He has already put a load in the washer: it is grinding away upstairs. Anna Banana remembers how hard Nathan worked all his life in the butcher shop, then the A&P when the butcher shop failed, and finally at the fish store that her brother

Eddie owned. Even after Nathan got sick he used to work six days a weeks, sometimes till nine at night.

Well, she thinks, Nathan worked too hard. That's all he did was work. No time for fun. No time for the children. Never went anywhere, never took her out. All work. Lois and David had fun, and that was good.

Nathan, Anna Banana thinks. Well, he didn't drink or fool with women, and he was a good provider.

～

Anna Banana eats breakfast. First she has juice and corn-flakes, and then she has eggs and toast. She has coffee and more toast before she feels full. For almost two years she wasn't hungry and lost over twenty pounds, then after Nathan died she got hungry again. And now she was always hungry, and ate and ate and didn't gain an ounce. All those diets she'd tried and they'd never worked, she had always gained weight, and now she ate all this food and gained nothing. It was crazy.

～

Right after breakfast, Anna Banana goes to the bathroom. She is never constipated anymore, and still has the bottle of Haley's M.O. that she brought with her from the city. She has only used it once since coming to Maine. She washes her face and cleans her false teeth and gets dressed, then puts on her apron and does the breakfast dishes. Her two jobs are dishes and taking the wash off the line, She used to make turkey loaf too, but the kids didn't like it.

When the dishes are finished, Anna Banana feels tired. She sits on the living room couch and looks out the window. There is nothing outside but trees and sky, no people or buildings or anything interesting, but it is restful and she sits there and stares a long time. She only stops staring when David comes down. She looks at her watch: an hour has passed, an hour of staring. Lois hates it when she stares, but David doesn't seem to mind.

David goes to the hallway and gets more plaster. "Keeping busy?" he asks as he walks through the room. "Oh yes," says

Anna Banana, and picks up a magazine. "I guess you'll hang out a wash today," she says. "Oh Christ," David says, "I forgot the wash, thanks for mentioning it," and Anna Banana feels good.

She reads *Time* magazine. She has finished the *Redbook* and *Ladies Home Journal.* When the *Time* magazine is finished she will have nothing new to read and will start on the *Redbook* again. She looks at the books on the shelf. *Classics in Linguistics.* She has looked at the books many times, but none of them are interesting.

∼

Eleven o'clock, and Anna Banana is hungry. She goes to the kitchen and makes a sandwich. There is nothing but peanut butter and cheese. She wishes there was roast beef. Corned beef would be better, but you can't get good corned beef in Maine. The next time she goes into town to get her hair done she will buy some roast beef.

She eats her cheese sandwich, then stands by the dining room window. It is twenty after eleven now, nearly time for the mailman to come. She goes back to the kitchen for cookies, then takes up her post at the window again. Eleven thirty comes, then twenty-five of twelve. He's late, she thinks. Then she thinks, Maybe he came early and I missed him, I better check, and she goes outside.

The sun is bright and the sky is a pure deep blue, but she doesn't notice. She is thinking about the mail. She walks quickly and almost stumbles. Why don't they cement this driveway, she thinks, how much would it cost? Her hand is shaking as she opens the mailbox door. The box is empty.

She starts back to the house. A breeze kicks up and she shivers. Cold, it's always cold here, why did they want to move where it's always cold? It's May and the leaves aren't even out, what a crazy place to live. Just as she reaches the door, the mail truck comes.

There's a newspaper in the box. It comes three times a week. Anna Banana unfolds it and looks inside. Three letters: David, David, Lois, and a thing from Sears. No check.

Tomorrow's the third, why didn't she get her check? I guess it will come tomorrow even though it's Saturday, she thinks. She has always gotten her check every month, they have never forgotten it yet.

David is eating his lunch when she goes back in. "Three letters," she says, and she gives them to him, but keeps the newspaper. "Bills," he says. "Just bills, heh?" she says, and sits down. She looks at the paper. "I was reading in that *Time* magazine about that woman—you know, the one that killed that movie star? When she met that man out there in California, the first thing he said to her was, 'Take off your clothes.'"

David looks at the bills. "Uh-huh."

"How about that?"

"Sounds like fun, huh, Anna?" David says, and Anna Banana laughs.

"Yeah," she says. She reads the paper.

Anna Banana is seventy-four. She reads the obituaries. Look at all the people who die in their eighties, she thinks. Nathan was eighty when he died. He would have been eighty-one in June, next month. It had happened so fast. He was perfectly healthy until he was seventy-eight, then just like that he got sick and then he was dead. In the hospital after he died all that Anna Banana had said was, "Such a good appetite, always asked for seconds," and Lois had looked at her, shaking her head. Well that was all she could think of to say, so she'd said it.

Nathan. What a life she had had with him. Poor Sam, he had died so young and he was so nice. She thinks about how things might have been with Sam. Well who could tell, maybe things would have been just as bad. After all, Nathan was nice when she met him, too. She almost never thought of Nathan now. When she did, she could only see him as he'd looked in Einstein, pale and yellow and hollow under his eyes. She had lived with him forty-five years, and whenever she thought of him now, that's how he looked.

~

David goes back to work and she reads the paper. She reads it from front to back, and when she is finished she sighs. There's nothing in it, she says to herself, it's always the same old stuff.

She thinks about Nathan again, of the way he looked, and the palpitation starts. It's mostly in her neck this time. That's not so bad. When it's in her chest, it's terrible. The vein keeps throbbing in her neck and she tells herself not to worry. She's had the palpitations for years and the doctors all say it is nothing.

She looks out the window and tries not to think about Nathan, but the throbbing won't stop. The last time she had it the pills made it better. She looks at her watch. One o'clock. Time to lay down for a while, she says to herself. She goes to the bathroom and swallows one of the pills.

She lies in bed and looks through the skylight—and the sky is gone. She wakes up with a start. For a second she thinks that someone is in her room. She is almost afraid to look, the feeling is so strong, but when she does look, no one is there. She lies staring out through the skylight, her heart beating fast. She is cold. The clock grinds away on the table beside the bed. Why does it make so much noise? she wonders. She sits up. She does not want to be in the room anymore. She goes to the bathroom and looks in the mirror. She looks at her neck, and the palpitation is gone.

~

"I guess the wash is dry now, heh?" she says.

David is in the hallway again. "It should be," he says.

"I'll bring it in."

Anna Banana gets the basket and goes outside. She makes her way around the garden and almost trips. The clothesline is high in the air and she jumps up to reach the clothes. She almost falls down and decides to lower the line. She loads her arms so full she can just about walk to the basket. What a job, she thinks. They have a dryer, why do they bother with this? Well, they do a lot of funny things. Some of the clothes fall onto the grass. Clumsy, she says to herself, I never do things right. She takes off the rest of the wash and goes back inside.

~

Anna Banana reads *Redbook* again and waits. At last the school bus comes and the children bang into the house. The little one goes upstairs to watch his father. The big one comes into the living room.

"What did you do in school today, Doug?" Anna Banana asks.

"I don't want to tell you," the child says.

"Come on, don't be like that. Tell me what you did in school."

"Anna Banana," the child says.

"Oh Dougie, don't call me that."

"Well what should I call you then?"

"Call me Grandmom."

"I like Anna Banana better."

"Don't tease me, Dougie, it isn't nice. Do you think it's nice to tease your grandmom?"

"Yes."

Anna Banana is quiet a minute. "How about a game of cards?" she says.

"Not today," Doug says. He has gotten his Lego set.

"I'll give you a piece of my chocolate candy," Anna Banana says.

The child hesitates. "Oh, all right," he says, and puts the Legos back.

They play crazy eights at the dining room table. Doug wins. He wants to play war, but she wants to play more crazy eights and they can't agree, so Doug gets his Legos again. The younger child comes down and sits at the table with a coloring book. As Anna Banana watches him color, she drums her fingers on the tabletop. "Shave and a haircut, two BITS!" she says as she drums. The child pays no attention. She drums her fingers again and smiles through perfect false teeth. "Dum dee dee dum-dum,

dum DUM! Can you do that, Mark? Watch me," and she drums again. The child puts his crayon down and imitates with a heavy banging. "Oh, don't do *that*," says Anna Banana. "You're so wild. Why are you so wild, Mark? Why don't you lay down and take a rest?"

The child makes an ugly face, and Anna Banana looks away. She looks out the window. "Oh, there's the flies again," she says.

"The flies?" the child says. "The *flies?*"

"The white flies. What do you call them?"

"The *butter*flies?"

"That's it, the butterflies. Look at them. Always out there."

The child picks up his coloring book and goes into the living room. Anna Banana follows him. It is almost four o'clock, and at four the children will turn on their shows and Anna Banana will watch them. She has her own TV in her room but she doesn't like sitting back there by herself. Anyway, the children's shows are pretty good, better than the other junk that's on. She checks her watch. Two minutes of four. Her stomach growls.

"What are we gonna have for dinner?" she asks the older child. He is building with Legos and doesn't answer. "What's Daddy making tonight?" Still no answer. "Maybe spaghetti," says Anna Banana. "Maybe pizza. I bet it's pizza."

"No," the child says, not looking up.

"What is it, then?" asks Anna Banana quietly. Her stomach rumbles again. She hopes they won't have that big scrambled egg in a bowl, sooflay or whatever they called it. Why didn't they ever eat meat? A butcher's daughter who doesn't eat meat, just chicken and turkey, whoever heard of such a thing? You needed meat to build red blood, didn't they know that? Well, you couldn't tell them anything. "Come on, Doug, tell me what we're having."

"Fish cakes!" the child shouts, and he bangs his fist on the floor.

"Fish cakes!" Anna Banana says with wide eyes, "Oh, they're *good*." In the city, she always got fish cakes at Kelley's. She used to get oysters at Kelley's too. "Oysters, french fries, pie and a cup of coffee," she says out loud.

"Fish cakes!" the child shouts again. There are tears in his eyes.

"Shh, not so loud," says Anna Banana. "Daddy will holler."

"He will not!"

"Oh yes he will. Listen, I hear him coming."

"You're dumb!" the child shouts.

Anna Banana's heart hurts. "Oh Doug, that isn't nice," she says. "Don't you love me?" She bends close to the child and asks again softly, "Dougie, don't you love me? You used to love me."

"Be quiet!" the child says. He jams his Legos into their box and turns the TV on.

~

When Lois comes home the children run and hug her. Anna Banana can smell the fish cakes cooking. Lois hangs her jacket up and Anna Banana says hello.

"Hello, Mother."

She looks so tired, Anna Banana thinks. Why doesn't David get a job? What did he go to college for? One thing about Nathan, he always worked hard. "Listen, Lois, I didn't get my check."

"It comes on the third," Lois says. "Tomorrow is the third."

"Tomorrow is Saturday," Anna Banana says. "Do they send them out on Saturdays?"

"You've gotten them on Saturdays before, haven't you?"

Anna Banana tries to think. She can't remember. "Oh, yeah, yeah, you're right," she says. "You're right, Lois."

Lois goes to the table and looks through the mail. David says hi from the kitchen; she goes in and gives him a kiss. Anna Banana watches the children's shows. She is the only one watching.

~

Anna Banana eats three fish cakes. They are pretty good. The rice is not so good, it is brown. Why did they eat brown rice when white rice was so much cheaper and so much better? "Brisket is good," she says. "Did you ever eat brisket?"

"Yes, Mother," Lois says.

"Well I know you ate it at home, but I mean now. Do you ever eat it now?"

"No," David says.

"Can't you get it in Maine?"

"You can get it," David says.

"Uh-huh," says Anna Banana, and she takes the last tomato.

"Mother," Lois says, "before you take the last tomato, could you ask if anyone else would like a piece?"

"Oh, I'm sorry," Anna Banana says. "Yeah, Lois, you're right." Why shouldn't I have the last tomato? she thinks. There are lots of of tomatoes left in their lives, why shouldn't I eat this one?

"Dishes, dishes, dishes," she says as she clears the table.

Lois sighs. "Mother, do we ask you to do so much around here?"

Anna Banana grins. "Lois, I'm only kidding, can't you take a joke? I'm only kidding."

"I don't like that kind of joke."

"All right, Lois, I'm sorry I said anything."

Anna Banana does the dishes, then watches the news. She sits on the couch with David as Lois gives the kids their baths. David sneezes. "God bless you," says Anna Banana. David doesn't seem to hear.

When the news is over, Anna Banana says, "David, I hate to bother you, but look at this thing on my arm." She has rolled up her sleeve.

"What thing?" David says. "This lump?"

"Oh my God," says Anna Banana, "don't say it's a lump. Oh David, don't say it's a lump."

David shrugs. "Well it looks like a lump to me. A lump, a bump, a hump, a bulge...call it whatever you want to call it, I don't care."

"Oh my God, it just can't be a lump."

"Well what do you mean?" David says. "Cancer? Is that what you think it is?"

"Oh my God, not cancer, oh Jesus, oh no, I don't mean Jesus, oh God."

"It isn't cancer, just get that out of your head."

"But you said it's a lump. A lump means cancer."

"Where did you ever hear that?"

"I read it in one of the magazines. Any lump, it said. Any lump."

"No, no, it's any lump that gets bigger or something. For Christ's sake, don't worry, it isn't cancer. Did you ever have varicose veins?"

She nods. "Years ago."

"Well that's what it looks like to me, a varicose vein, but if you're worried about it, we'll see a doctor."

"Oh no, I'm sure it's nothing," says Anna Banana. "I was just curious, that's all." She rolls down her sleeve and buttons it and looks at the TV again.

Mark comes in shining, his hair freshly combed, and she asks him to go get her watch, which she's left in the kitchen. Mark makes a face but gets the watch and gives it to her. "Thanks, sweetheart, aren't you good," she says. "I'm lost without my watch." Mark makes another face and leaves the room.

～

Anna Banana watches the Lawrence Welk show. Look at the old folks, she says to herself. Old folks like me. You get old so fast. She remembers that time she saw Al Jolson and Fannie Brice in person at Steel Pier. It was long ago, long before Lois was born, but somehow it doesn't seem that long ago. She wonders how old Lawrence Welk is now. He still looks pretty good. But didn't she read somewhere that he was dead?

When the show ends, Anna Banana is tired. It is seven thirty. The children are drawing at the dining room table and David and Lois are talking, and she says goodnight. She goes to the bathroom and cleans her teeth, puts on her nightgown and gets into bed. It is still light outside. She looks at the skylight awhile, then looks at the lump on her arm. The way David said that, *It isn't cancer,* making her feel so dumb. So how does he know it isn't cancer, is he a doctor?

If only Lois had married a doctor. She wonders whatever became of that nice obstetrician. Well, that was a long time ago. She looks at the lump in the dying light. She had better go see a doctor. Maybe when she got her hair done next time. Lois could make both appointments for the same day.

~

In her dream she is thirty-six. She is married to Sam; he owns a chain of supermarkets in Miami. She has her own place to live in again, and it is a beautiful place. She sits in the sun on the terrace and looks at the beach.

Lois is down by the water, making castles out of sand. She stops for a minute and waves. Anna Banana waves back. The comforting water shines in the distance as far as her eyes can see. The maid brings a nice cold drink and some butter creams, and Anna Banana leans back in her lounge chair with her *Collier's* magazine. The sun is warm on her shoulders and legs, and she looks at Lois and smiles.

Mistakes

They spent the whole day on Blue Island again, working on Lullworth, the cottage owned by the mail order clothing people. Most of the time Jake was up on the roof, but the last thing he did was help get the furnace into the cellar. Lullworth had eight large bedrooms and four full baths, and the furnace was huge: each of its cast iron sections weighed six hundred pounds. What a job, you could goddamn kill yourself.

At home in the trailer's cramped steel shower Jake's whole body ached, then his tooth started up again. It had hurt in the morning and then eased off, but now it was really a jeezer. At supper it hurt so much he hardly spoke to Kelly. After he finished his hamburger helper he opened a second beer and went to his rocker and turned the ballgame on; drank quickly, hoping to dull his pain.

The Red Sox were playing Seattle. The game was in the top of the third and the Sox were two runs down. "Hopeless," Jake said, leaning back in his chair.

Kelly was still in the kitchen and didn't hear.

"They started off so good this year. Even a couple of weeks ago it looked like they had a chance."

"What?" Kelly said. She was now in the doorway, a slant of low sunlight striking her coppery hair. Her mother and both of her brothers had that hair. It made Jake think of the wire brush he used to clean the pickup's battery posts.

"The Red Sox started off so good," he said, "and now the same old thing. Middle of August, they're eight games back."

"Too bad," Kelly said, coming into the narrow room.

She wasn't a baseball fan. Jake didn't know why he bothered to talk to her about the games. He just felt like talking about them sometimes, and she was there.

Kelly sat on the couch, on its zebra-striped vinyl, and picked up the *Woman's Day* she had bought that afternoon at the Shop 'N Save. She would read for a while and then she would wash the dishes, and Jake would dry. When he looked at her now, he wondered again if the baby would have her hair.

He drank his beer, a Rolling Rock. He liked Sam Adams best, but it cost too much, was only for special occasions. He held the green bottle up to the light of the pair of aluminum windows. Almost gone, and his tooth was still throbbing. How many beers would it take to knock it down?

He leaned back again in the rocker. My God did he hurt: his tooth, his shoulders, his back, his neck, his thighs. At least he hadn't mashed his thumb, like Walt Cummings. One of the cast iron furnace sections had slipped and pinned old Walt against the jamb, and man had he yelled. He'd be out for at least a month.

The tooth had been giving Jake trouble for weeks. He needed a root canal and crown, the dentist said, but where the hell would he get the money for that? If it didn't calm down he'd have it pulled, that's all he could afford. He'd probably be like the old man and lose all his teeth by the time he was thirty. Goddamn.

He tilted his head back, drank and watched the Sox. Then suddenly he sat straight up and said, "What? What? you're kidding me!"

"What's wrong?" Kelly said.

"I don't believe this! Jesus!"

"*What?*" Kelly said. Annoyance in her voice—and worry, too.

"It's Milligan. Rick Milligan."

"Who's that?"

"He's playing for Seattle, second base."

"Yeah? So?"

"I played with him," Jake said. "I played *against* him, and then I played *with* him."

He set the bottle down on the coffee table; blond formica, two wet rings. The camera zoomed in on the batter's face: black hair, black eyebrows knit in a scowl.

"It's him, all right. I haven't seen him for—Christ, twelve years, but it's him. Jesus Christ."

The pitcher threw and Milligan swung and cracked a line drive to center.

"He got a hit," Jake said. "He got a friggin' hit."

"So Milligan, called up from triple A two weeks ago, continues to be hot," the announcer said. "This gives him fifteen hits in forty-three trips to the plate." "And he's done a fine job at second, too," the other announcer said.

"Second base," Jake said. "He played short on the All-Stars. Huh. There he goes."

"He's in there," the announcer said. "That's Milligan's fourth stolen base since he's been called up, they haven't caught him yet."

"Oh he's quick," Jake said. "He's quick all right." He reached for his bottle and drained it.

"Fastest kid on the All-Star team. And I was next, just a little bit slower. Not much."

"When was this?" Kelly said.

"Little League," Jake said. "Twelve years ago. His team and mine were the best in the league. We had a playoff game to decide the championship, I was the pitcher—"

"And that's in the gap, it's off the wall, and here comes Milligan in to score."

Jake went to the kitchen and got a fresh bottle of beer. Came back, sat down in his chair again. "I struck him out," he said.

"Twelve years ago."

"Yeah. He was the league's best player, and I was the second best. The playoff game was the third time our teams had met that year. I didn't pitch the other games, and we lost them both. But they had lost to a team that we beat twice, so we had the playoff."

"So after two and a half," the announcer said, "it's the Mariners three, the Red Sox nothing." An ad for athletic shoes came on.

Jake drank some beer. His face was feeling a little numb and his tooth didn't hurt so bad. "The first time up against me, he got a hit. A single off a fastball, and then he stole second. Quick, he was quick. I got the rest of the side out, though. The next time, I nibbled at him and walked him. He stole again, and this time he scored, and the game was tied. And then in the sixth, which is all the innings you have in Little League ball, I walk two guys and Milligan comes to the plate. I throw him a fastball and man does he hit it—but foul. Strike one. I throw him a ball in the dirt. Then a fastball high and tight and he swings—and ticks it off. Strike two. He stares at me like he wants to kill me. You never saw a kid who was so intense."

As he talked, Jake watched the TV screen. The Sox had a guy on first.

"So then it was time for the pitchfork change. My old man had taught it to me. You hold the ball with the middle three fingers, press down with the index finger, and throw with the fastball motion." He demonstrated for Kelly, who looked confused. "I had to have luck to get it over, but this was the time to use it.

"And I had luck. It was perfect, right down the middle. Milligan was out in front, *way* out in front, and you never saw a kid so mad. He ground his teeth and held both ends of the bat and brought it straight down on his helmet. Three times, his face all red. Our stands went wild. I felt like—unbelievable. I got Rick Milligan! I caught a look at my dad, and what a grin. He wasn't a guy who smiled much, but he smiled then."

"And you won?" Kelly said.

"We lost," Jake said. "The next kid hit one to center that shoulda been caught, but it went all the way to the fence and they scored and won."

"Too bad."

"But I got Rick Milligan," Jake said, "and now here he is. Here he *is*."

He drank. The alcohol was in his muscles; his shoulders felt warm and smooth. "So we played on the Little League All-Stars together," he said. "He played short and I pitched. When I didn't pitch, I played right field. I won two games. One game I struck out twelve, walked two, and gave up only one hit. At the states, I pitched the opening game and won it with a double in the sixth—drove Milligan home. At the plate he gave me high fives and a hug, we were happy dudes. But we lost the next two games and that was it, and I never saw him again."

"How come?"

"He moved. His dad got a job in Boston. For a year or so I heard stuff about him. Somebody said he got hurt and couldn't play ball down there. Somebody said he quit baseball for football. Time went by and I never heard anything else."

He drank more beer and watched the game. A ball was hit to Milligan. He scooped it up and tossed to the bag for the force and the Sox were gone.

"Goddamn," Jake said.

"What," Kelly said.

"Oh nothing, forget it."

The commercial this time concerned beer. Jake ran his finger around the rim of his bottle; a small nick there. "They actually took a look at me when I was a senior," he said. "It was almost unheard of, who bothers with class C schools in Maine? This Red Sox scout, Johnny Feather, a pretty old guy, he checked Billy Donovan out my freshman year. Never saw him again, then here I am three years later, a senior, I come back in after four strong innings, the coach says, 'Lookin' good. You see Johnny Feather up there?'

"I spotted him right away. He had sunglasses on and was holding a clipboard. I took the mound again and I was *shaking*—walked the first two guys. A typical wild lefty, he's gonna think, I told myself. But that wasn't me, I had good control.

"So their clean-up hitter is next. He takes the first pitch right down the middle, strike one. On the next one, another fastball, he swings and misses. My old man had taught me a roundhouse curve after Little League when my arm matured, and I thought, yeah, that's what I'll throw. But then I thought, he'll look for the curve, I should throw him the pitchfork change. My catcher gives me the sign for the curve, low and outside. Waste pitch, try to make him fish. Okay.

"But I make a mistake and get it up. I hang the goddamn thing. Lots of times it wouldn't matter, lots of high school kids can't hit the curve no matter what, but this kid could. He rips it down the line for a double and two runs score. I was shaking so much I walked the next batter. And Feather left, just got up and left. I felt sick to my stomach, but struck out the side. We ended up winning, four to two, and I was seven and 0. But I blew it. When it counted, I blew it.

"Dad had stopped coming to games by then, and I never told him what happened. He'd lost a lot of weight and was always so tired and sad, and I just didn't want him to know. I pitched three more games and won them all, but Feather never came back."

The Mariners were out, the Sox were up. "Well nobody drafts a kid out of class C ball anyway," Jake said. "The best kid I ever saw was Billy Donovan, he hit .510 with six home runs, he was six foot three, two hundred and fifteen pounds and Feather said no."

Jake used the bathroom, then went to the fridge for another beer. He was getting a pretty good buzz on now. The pain in his tooth was tiny and far away, but God he was tired. He went back into the living room. "Jesus Christ," he said, "the Sox are already out?"

"I wasn't paying attention," Kelly said.

Jake sat again, put his feet on the coffee table. "Pathetic." His sneaker hid one of the cigarette burns. He said, "I got a base-ball scholarship."

"To Farmington."

"Yeah, Farmington. You know all this."

"You were tired of school."

"I wanted to make some money. And I couldn't leave Mom alone with Dad, it wasn't right."

"So you started at Seacoast."

"Yeah." Jake drank; he watched the screen. "I shoulda played Legion ball, I guess, but Dad was so sick, and the closest team was Augusta. To drive an hour there and back four days a week after working all day... Dad thought I should do it, but I don't know, he couldn't come to the games and it just didn't seem important anymore."

Jake looked at the green and white bottle, frowning. Once he had found a dime in a bottle of beer.

"Billy Donovan played Legion ball," he said. "He hit like a terror and finally he *did* get drafted. By Cleveland. He lasted half a year in the rookie league. I looked at him and thought, If *he* can't do it..."

Squeezing the bottle's neck, he drank. "I was small, too small," he said, "five-nine. You can make it at second, or maybe the outfield, but not as a pitcher. Everyone told me that, so I checked all my baseball cards, and sure enough, all the pitchers were over six foot. I could hit, but an outfielder has to *really* hit, so what other choice does a leftie have? First base? A five foot nine first baseman? Gimme a break. He's up again."

The screen was hazy now, its colors blurred. "Milligan's five-ten, a hundred and eighty-five pounds," the announcer said. "A real pleasant surprise for Seattle since replacing the injured Evans."

"Five-ten," Jake said. "An inch taller than me. One lousy inch, and we weigh the same."

"And there's another hit for Milligan," the announcer said. "So the Mariners have the leadoff runner on base again."

"Five-ten," Jake said. "One lousy inch. But he plays second base. I stopped growing in tenth grade, and maybe I shoulda stuck to the outfield and worked on my hitting, who knows, but I loved to pitch. And who the hell from a class C school ever thinks they can make the show? But I was as good as Milligan." He drank. "Almost."

Without looking at Kelly, he said, "You remember the fair last year, the radar gun?"

She didn't reply at first, then, "Oh, that pitching thing?"

"That pitching thing."

"You did pretty good," she said.

Jake drank, and now he looked at her. "Pretty good," he said. "Ninety-two miles an hour, three times. Three out of four times, ninety-two miles an hour. That's big league speed, but they don't care, you're five foot nine, forget it."

"Milligan's heading for second, and...he's safe! That's twice in a row he's stolen off Ford." "This kid is impressive, Sal, he gets a real good jump..."

"I struck him out," Jake said. He was standing now, holding the bottle with just two fingers, holding its rim, his arm at his side. "I struck the fucker out."

"Jake! Watch your language!"

Jake rolled his eyes. What the hell did she think, the baby could hear him? "Well that's how it is," he said. He set his bottle down on the coffee table, stared at it. His tooth was starting up again. "Some smartass guy on TV said opportunity doesn't knock only once, it keeps on knocking. Not in baseball, it doesn't." He sniffed. "You know damn well that Milligan doesn't live in some beat-up trailer and eat goddamn hamburger helper three times a week."

Kelly frowned, looking hurt. "We won't *always* live in a trailer. And you *like* hamburger helper, that's why I make it."

"I goddamn better like it," Jake said, and went to the door.

"Where are you going?"

"Outside."

When they'd moved to the trailer he'd nailed a coffee can to the front of the tumbledown barn, waist high, its mouth pointing at him like a cannon. And this time of year when the old summer apple tree started to drop its fruit, he'd come out and throw at the can. Mostly fastballs, but sometimes curves and changeups too.

Last night it had stormed and now there were plenty of apples lying around in the grass. He picked up a fat one and heaved it hard. Missed, not even close. Another fastball, strike! then two more misses. A curve. A miss. Well the beer sure as hell didn't help your control.

His eyes were heavy and hot and the tooth was really picking up steam. He'd have to get it yanked. Goddamn. He threw again, hit the edge of the can and the apple was sliced in two.

Billy Donovan hadn't made it. He'd come closer than anyone else, but he hadn't made it, and now what the hell did he do? Drove a garbage truck.

"They drafted him out of Legion ball," Jake said aloud, "and what good did it do? He still didn't make it." Another miss. "So was that a mistake? Not playing Legion ball that summer? Not going away to Farmington when Dad was dying?" He threw, hit the can.

"And when Feather was in the stands, that curve, of all times to hang it, damn, I shoulda thrown the change."

Turning an apple around and around in his hand, he said, "No one thinks they can do it. You go to a class C school in Maine, two hundred and thirty-eight kids, even Donovan didn't believe it. And Christ, when you're only five foot nine... Maybe that was my biggest mistake, being born too small." He threw again and missed again. The apple splattered hard on the splintered boards.

"But Milligan *made* it. Five-ten and he friggin' *made* it. Yeah, but he got *away* from here."

Jake looked around. The light on the tangled field behind the barn was sullen bronze, like the end of the world was waiting just over the ridge.

This place. He'd hoped to be out of here before winter,

before the baby came, but no money, they spent every penny they earned. Kelly would quit at Wal-Mart soon and then...Jesus Christ. "What the hell does he make a week?" Jake said. "He makes thousands, they all do, even the rookies." Staring at the can's bent rim he threw again. It was wide to the left, and burst into mush.

"What can I tell her?" he said to the patchy grass and gnarled tree. "That I still play ball in my dreams? Can I tell her that?" He picked up more apples.

Tomorrow he'd go to Blue Island again and work on the rich people's cottage. "Well that's how it is," he said to himself, looking down at his hand. An ant had crawled out of an apple; he crushed it to death with the heel of his palm. "Yeah, that's how it is."

He'd go to Blue Island and work on the rich people's roof. And Milligan would play for Seattle, that's how all the days would go, and now when he looked at the can on the wall he pictured Rick Milligan, cocky and glaring, confident in his Mariner's blue, and reared back and fired, pure heat, three strikes in a row.

Journey

Now someone was suddenly right in front of her, blurred, a ghost, and Wilma caught her breath. Her hands went tight on the rails of her walker.

"Hi, Mrs. Potter," a musical voice said. "It's Annie, how are you doing?"

Annie. The new one, the young one, who'd only come twice before, the one who called her "Mrs. Potter." Wilma's frightened heart began to slow. "Oh, I'm all right," she said.

Her ears were very bad now, almost as bad as her eyes. If she wasn't right there at the kitchen table, next to the door that went out to the shed, she couldn't hear people knock. She'd bought some hearing aids but they didn't work, just whistled and buzzed, and she never wore them.

Olive had always barked like mad when anyone came to the door. Wilma could always hear that fine, but now poor Olive was gone. The door was never bolted shut, and after the people knocked they came right in, scaring Wilma to death. It couldn't be helped, but she hated it, couldn't get used to it, probably never would.

"How's your hip, Mrs. Potter?"

"Not great," Wilma said. "Damp out, I guess."

"It's raw, the weather report says snow,"

"What?"

"THE WEATHER REPORT SAYS SNOW."

"Oh, yes, well, my hip is my weather report."

It was over a year since she'd fallen and broken her hip and had it replaced. It still throbbed at night a lot of the time and on damp cold days. As she clumped toward the table it sent shooting pains through her thigh.

"Can you see where the chair is?" Annie asked.

"What?"

"THE CHAIR. CAN YOU SEE YOUR CHAIR?"

"I can see it."

Just barely. She didn't know why she bothered to wear her glasses, the darn things were worthless, just like those hearing aids. She guessed she was used to them, liked how they felt on her nose, but they didn't work. The world was all blurry, and then when she reached for something it wasn't where she thought it was. The nurses wanted to take her down for another exam, but she wouldn't go. What was the point? Dr. Adams said nothing would help, her veins were shot in the back of her eyes. She couldn't read, the TV was nothing but squiggles and smears, she couldn't see faces. The nurses all looked the same to her—except for their size. This Annie was pretty small.

Wilma stopped, clutching the walker, and let out a breath. The trip across the kitchen had worn her out. Most of her life she had worked from morning to night, now a twenty foot walk wore her out. But she wouldn't let on to the aides, they might start with that Seaview business. So what if she was ninety-five and damn near deaf and blind? As long as she could move, she'd stay right here at home. She'd lived here over sixty years and even if her eyes went all the way she'd be able to get around, she knew every inch of the place.

"Let's do your blood pressure," Annie said.

Wilma looked at her out of the sides of her eyes. She could see just a bit out of one tiny spot, her TV spot, and she saw Annie's nose. She lost it again as the blood pressure cuff tightened up on her arm. Tighter, tighter, then looser again, and Annie said, "It's a little high. Not bad, but a little high."

"What?"

"I SAID IT'S A LITTLE HIGH."

"Oh. Must be all the excitement around this place."

Annie laughed. "I guess."

"I take my pills."

"I know you do. And there's no need to change anything, we'll just keep an eye on the situation."

"An eye," Wilma said. "What I wouldn't give for one good eye."

Her pills were on the table in a board with holes drilled into it. The nurses came and put the pills in the holes three days a week. Her fingers were bad, but Wilma could feel which holes were which. Aside from the blood pressure pills there were pills for her heart, her kidneys, her lungs, her circulation, her swollen ankles, arthritis and diabetes. She was sick to death of the pills, but she took them.

"Pulse is good," Annie said. "Any complaints?"

"What?"

"ANY COMPLAINTS?"

Not a one, Wilma thought. *I love living like this.* "I'm fine," she said. "Just my hip acting up in bad weather."

"Good thing you had that furnace put in last year," Annie said. "Trying to keep that woodstove going would be quite a challenge with your hip."

"Well, yes," Wilma said, "but I never get really warm with oil. It blows the heat then stops, then blows and stops, and every time it stops the house cools off again. With wood I was always warm. You feed that old Home Comfort sticks of oak and maple and you get a steady heat, a heat you can control. I never could understand the big thing about oil. We haul it in from foreign countries that hate us, when wood's the best fuel in the world and it's right in our own back yard."

"Good point," Annie said. "But with your hip and arthritis and vision problem it's hard to manage a woodstove."

"Hard to manage a thermostat too."

"I see somebody marked it."

"What?"

"I SEE SOMEBODY MARKED IT."

"They marked it with thick red stuff I can't see or feel,"

Wilma said. "My eyes are no good and my fingers are dead. I just leave it on 78."

"That works okay for you?"

"What?"

"THAT'S OKAY FOR YOU?"

"Yeah, it's okay. I don't want to turn it higher, I'd be too warm. And it might blow up."

"I don't think so."

"What?"

"I SAID I DON'T THINK SO."

"It might. It happened to Alice Farnham, covered her walls with soot. Oil soot, my lord what a mess. With a woodstove you don't have to worry about that stuff."

"You don't ever use it, do you? You still have some wood in that wagon there."

These people were constantly worried about her trying to use the Home Comfort again, thought she'd burn herself up. She didn't even use the electric stove, just the microwave, but they had to ask. "That wood in the wagon's in case of emergency," she said. "I don't trust machines too much."

"I like the wagon."

"What?"

"IT'S A NICE LITTLE WAGON."

The wagon was red. Had been bright red to begin with, then darkened with time, and now, to Wilma, it looked brown. All reds looked brown. "That wagon belonged to one of my boys," she said. "I guess it's an antique, now. Like me, like everything else in this place. I hauled my wood in that wagon for years. I put those bricks on the floor when my eyes got bad, let me know when to stop the wagon."

"Clever," Annie said. "Mrs. Potter, you're something. Living way up on this hill all alone with no people around."

"Oh, I'm something, all right," Wilma said. "An antique. I miss my wood. I guess I'd like oil okay if I lived in a tight little trailer, but here in this big old house..."

A few years back, she'd had a plan. She'd try to sell the house to some rich outtastaters who wanted a country place in Maine, and keep half an acre or so past the pond and put a new trailer on it. She'd still be able to live on the land she loved, but not have to fool with the house—or pay taxes on over a hundred acres.

But no outtastaters wanted to fool with the old house either. It needed new clapboards and cellar stairs, a new living room ceiling, a roof. It even needed sills, foundation work, new windows, doors...what *didn't* it need? No one had worked on the place since Gerald died, and that was over forty years ago. Hard to believe all that time had gone by. So fast.

The barn was collapsing, its back wall was curved like the prow of a ship. Outtastaters would tear it down. Would tear the house down too, no doubt, build new. And nobody wanted a crippled old lady living next door in a trailer, it was depressing. The sale sign fell over during a storm years back and Wilma never picked it up. For all she knew, it was still lying there.

"They blew in some insulation when they put in the furnace, didn't they?" Annie asked.

"What?"

"INSULATION? THEY BLEW INSULATION IN?"

"Oh yes," Wilma said. "In the attic. I was supposed to get storm windows too, in the kitchen, but then all their funding ran out. I can't complain, it was all for free. Even built that new cinder block chimney for free. I didn't like taking charity, but I needed help."

"These services are in place for people who need them," Annie said. "Don't think of them as charity."

The girl was trying to make her feel better, but who was she telling how to think? Charity was charity. Her SSI was charity. She'd mostly worked right here on the farm and didn't qualify for Social Security, and now that she was poor and old, she got SSI. Thank God. Without it she'd have no money at all. But it was still charity.

"You worked very hard all your life and deserve these things," Annie said.

"I suppose," Wilma said.

A knock on the door then and Annie said, "Here's your Meals on Wheels."

The door from the woodshed came open and someone walked in, a man. He looked like a moving pillar of fuzz as he placed a styrofoam box on the table. "Hi, Wilma," he said. She could hear him, he had a strong voice. "Tryin' to beat this jeezer of a storm that's comin', gotta run. Stay warm." He left again, closing the door. Its glass pane shook.

"I never remember that one's name," Wilma said. "There's three of them come, there's Ed and Mitchell, but this one I can't remember."

"I don't know them yet," Annie said. "I'm too new on the job."

"Well how 'bout you open that up and let's see what we got."

Annie opened the styrofoam box.

"I can't see it, you'll have to tell me," Wilma said.

"It's meatloaf and mashed potatoes and peas."

"You said meatloaf?"

"Yes."

"Good, their meatloaf's one of my favorites. Some of the stuff they give you, the fish, for instance... I guess you shouldn't look a gift horse in the mouth, but that fish is like rubber. I used to make meatloaf every week, my husband and boys just loved it."

"I'll bet they did. Can I get you a fork?"

"What?"

"A FORK?"

"They're in that white cabinet beside the ice box, top drawer."

As Annie crossed the room to the cabinet, the window beside the table suddenly rattled. "Just listen to that," Wilma said. "Even I can hear that."

"The wind's really kicking up," Annie said, coming back. She placed the fork on the table. "Before you start eating, how 'bout I check your Communicaid."

She pushed a button on the front of the small rectangular box that hung around Wilma's neck and it gave off a beep. "Fine," she said. "You warm enough? You want me to button that sweater?"

"Please," Wilma said. "My hands don't work so good anymore, my fingertips... They say it's the diabetes."

Annie began at the bottom. "Leave that top one open," Wilma said. "It chokes me when I'm lying down."

"How's this? Okay?"

"Just right."

"Your fork's there next to the box."

Wilma groped for it, missed it, hit the phone. She heard the clang it made.

"Here, let me help you," Annie said, and picked up the fork and put it in Wilma's hand.

"What a bother I am," Wilma said. "These eyes of mine, things jump all over the place. I'd be lost without all you people, I can't even open a jar half the time, the lids are so tight. That opener under the cabinet works, not always though." She shook her head. "Okay, let's see what I can hit."

She lowered the fork. "Feels like potatoes." She put them into her toothless mouth. Soft and tepid, tasted fake.

"There's a small cup of apple juice too," Annie said. "Let me open it for you."

"Oh, thank you, dear."

"Can you see it?"

"I see it."

"You know what you're having for supper tonight?"

"What?"

"WHAT ARE YOU HAVING FOR SUPPER TONIGHT?"

"For supper?"

"YES."

"Just cereal, it suits me fine."

"Okay. Your pills are set up for tomorrow. Linda will be here Friday and give you your bath."

Wilma heard that okay. Her bath, how she hated her bath. They were always so eager to clean her up, like she'd die if she didn't get washed. Some time ago, when colors still looked okay, she'd watched a TV show about old people, and there was a man who was over a hundred, down in South America somewhere, who hadn't taken a bath in a dozen years. That might be going a bit too far, but it proved the point. She hated help with her bath. Who wouldn't?

"You be here again next week?" she said.

"Next week I'm off, it's my vacation."

"Going someplace warm, I hope."

"As a matter of fact, I am—to Florida."

"Did you say Florida?"

"That's right."

"To Florida," Wilma said. "That's nice. My husband was going to take me there. 'One of these days when we save enough, we'll go on a journey, Wilma. South, to Florida, stay for a month, get away from this cold for a while.' That's what he told me, but then he got hurt and we couldn't go. We spent all our money on doctor bills and couldn't afford it."

"Oh, what a shame," Annie said.

"We were payin' off doctor bills for years, we didn't have any insurance. Thank God I have Medicaid now. So you have a wonderful time down there. Eat an orange for me."

"I will," Annie said with a little laugh. "Is there anything else you need right now before I leave?"

"What's that?"

"IS THERE ANYTHING ELSE I CAN DO?"

"Well, yes, could you put that trash bag out? The box is out front, near the door."

"Of course."

The window shook again as Annie lifted the bag from the green plastic trash can that stood near the table.

"Too bad they ran out of money before I could get those storm sash," Wilma said. "At least they put that plastic sheeting up. That plastic banking helps out too. That wind was whippin' across the floor till they tacked that up. Free oil, yeah, they did a lot for me. Don't think I don't appreciate it."

"I know you do," Annie said, now holding the bag of trash.

"With what I get, the SSI, I can't afford people to work for me."

"Of course you can't. Well, I have to get going. Enjoy your lunch. I'll see you the week after next."

"Thank you, dear."

The kitchen door opened then closed and the girl was gone. The house was quiet, except for the window, which rattled again. Wilma shivered.

She finished her meal. The peas were undercooked. The meatloaf was okay, the same as always, but not really good. The meatloaf she used to make! And the applesauce, from Macs and Northern Spies and Jonathans. The food they used to grow! "No matter how rich a person is, they can't buy food like ours," her Gerald used to say. "How many people in New York City have ever tasted a really good apple pie?" So much good food, fresh in the summer and canned the rest of the year. Those shelves down cellar stacked with jars of tomatoes and beets and carrots and string beans and raspberries, pickles—you name it. Apples and turnips and squash and potatoes in bins...

Those shelves and bins were empty now. She hadn't been down that cellar in years, couldn't manage the stairs. A good part of her house—the cellar, the attic, the whole second floor— was unavailable to her. She'd almost certainly never see them again.

She hadn't even left the kitchen more than a couple of times since she broke her hip. Didn't need to, really. The bathroom was off the kitchen, her bed was here, her TV was right on the table. Convenient, but awful boring to be in the same old room all the time. Well, no worse than a trailer.

She finished the applesauce. Insipid stuff. She wished she could taste a jar of the applesauce she used to make, to tell if it was the sauce or her tongue to blame for the blandness of all her food.

Had the girl put a new plastic bag in the trash can? The top of the can was white, so she must have, yes. Wilma picked up the styrofoam box, reached out. The can was more to the left than she'd thought. She tried to see through that little good spot, her TV spot, but it was so doggone small. *Oh well, here goes.*

She opened her bony fist and released the box. Bullseye. Thank God. She hated it when she missed—and with these foolish eyes of hers, she missed a lot.

It was time for her nap, and after that her TV stories, then her cereal, the news, then bed. And sleep right quick if she was lucky, otherwise the loneliness. An aching hip or aching hands could keep her up in the empty darkness, lost in memories. She hated that.

Why in the world did she go on living? She couldn't see, she couldn't hear, she couldn't go anywhere. All the people she'd ever cared about were dead: her husband, her sons, her sister, her neighbors, her friends. No one remembered her family. Nobody knew her history. Time had erased all the people she'd known, had erased her past, and now was erasing her. *Well let it erase me then,* she'd think as she lay on the little bed by the bathroom door. *Let it erase me all the way.* But it never did.

On that TV program about old people they showed where these—what were they, Arabs?—went into the hills with their goats in the summer and back to the valleys in winter. They had to wade across this river. Anyone too weak to wade across was left on the bank to die. The man they left on the bank when she watched the show looked healthier than ˊanyone down to Seaview. That was a better way of living, maybe, better than this endless patching up and going on.

Well, she wasn't an Arab, and this just wasn't her time. God didn't want her yet. —If indeed there was a God who cared at all about things of this earth. When Bobby had died she was certain there was no God. Then later she thought that there must be a God or life didn't make any sense at all. Now she didn't know what she thought, but it didn't matter. What mattered was that winter was here again with its short cold days. Her ninety-fifth winter, and every last one of them spent in the State of Maine.

Don't think about Bobby, she told herself as she struggled up into her walker. She thought about Bobby every day, she couldn't help it, *but please, not now, some other time, it's time for your nap.*

She inched her way slowly across to the bed and lowered herself to the mattress. Took off her no-good glasses and put them down on the nightstand, beside the clock. She felt like taking the thing at her neck off too, the Communicaid, but didn't. She lay on her side then, facing the room.

The furnace down cellar, below the floorboards that held this bed, switched on again, she could feel the vibration. The kitchen had two registers, one by the window and one by the door. The bathroom had one too. The air began to warm up, slowly, thinly. Wood heat was different, penetrating, made your body glow; this stuff was there for a little while then gone. Oh well, it was safe, and the pipes wouldn't freeze since the duct-work warmed the cellar.

Her hip was throbbing now. Not bad, she thought it wouldn't keep her up. She thought she heard the window shake again, but wasn't sure. She hoped it wasn't the door. She didn't see anyone over there. She could see the table and window, all blurred, the Home Comfort, the wagon a muddy smear. She'd probably never pull that wagon again.

Well, maybe she would. When her nap was finished, maybe she'd pull that wagon just for the heck of it, pull it a couple of feet toward the door, then back again. Just for the heck of it, pull Bobby's wagon. *Not Bobby again,* she told herself, *not now...*

~

When she woke, she thought she was up in the bedroom, up in the big maple bed. She was insubstantial, an apparition, a wraith. Then the pains asserted themselves again and it came to her where she was and who she was. *I'm still alive,* she thought.

The room was much darker than when she had shut her eyes. Either that or her eyes were suddenly worse. Had she dreamed? She couldn't remember.

She pulled herself up. Her shoulders hurt, her neck, her back, her knees. Across the room the window clattered angrily. The wind had always made the windows whine on stormy days. She didn't hear that anymore. Maybe the plastic sheets across the glass had toned it down; maybe her ears were too far gone to pick up sounds like that. When she sat at the table, right next to the window, she thought she could hear that whine sometimes, but sometimes it sounded like voices. She never told anyone that, they might send her to Seaview. Not just for rehab, like before, when she broke her hip, but for good.

"Extended care facility," they called it now, they had all kinds of therapies, but it was still an old age home. She'd visited Charlotte Perkins, her last living friend, in Seaview. One time she went before Halloween, and the walls and windows were decorated with cutouts of Jack-O-Lanterns and witches' hats and ghosts. It was just like a third grade classroom. How sorry she'd felt for poor Charlotte, who'd been Dr. Carr's receptionist for more than thirty years. Wilma had vowed right then and there that no one was going to turn her into a child.

Her knuckles hurt, and her wrists. She felt for her glasses and put them on, then picked up the clock on the nightstand. *Careful, careful,* her fingers so numb she was always dropping things. Her hands were shaking. They always shook. The numbers on the clock were huge, two inches high. She knew they were red, but they didn't look red, they looked brown. She could just about make them out.

Three forty-six! Could that be right? She squinted hard through her little good spot. Yes, three forty-six, she had slept for over two hours and missed two stories and part of a third. Not that it mattered much. You could miss a whole week and it wouldn't much matter.

She switched on the nightstand's lamp and its glow made her feel a bit better. She had to use the bathroom now, and grabbed the walker's rails and hoisted herself. Her knees and artificial hip complained.

Slowly she edged toward the bathroom door and the walker's feet hit the threshold. She grabbed the rail that Community Action had screwed to the wall, moved the walker aside. Worked the switch and the overhead light came on.

To her left was the tub. Straight ahead was the sink. To the left of that, at the end of the tub, was the toilet. She found the sink, held on, and turned around.

A hook between the toilet and sink held her towel. She took her Communicaid off and put its cord over the hook, on top of the towel. This way it wouldn't fall into the toilet again. How embarrassing that had been! She thought for sure they'd say she was ready for Seaview.

When she sat, the Communicaid was at shoulder height, within easy reach. It was wonderful having it off. She felt like a criminal with it on, like one of those people the cops kept track of. She needed it, she knew she did, but hated the foolish thing. Twice she had triggered it accidentally, making the hospital call. She apologized, but they said no problem, people did that all the time. They were glad to hear her voice. If she hadn't answered the phone, they'd have sent someone out.

She was always worried that someone would barge right into the kitchen and catch her here on the toilet. She never bothered to close the bathroom door when she was alone. *Probably wouldn't even know if someone was here or not,* she thought as she finished, and flushed, and stood, and reached for the sink—and the sink wasn't there.

No sink! She'd missed it! Shock, alarm—and then she fell.

On her hip, hard, right on her hip! Not the hip she had fallen on before, her other one, the good one. The pain was as bad as that other fall and she knew right away that the hip was broken. She'd broken her other hip! The pain was gigantic, was overwhelming, shot through her side, her back, *my God...* She moaned. My God, she'd broken her other hip, they'd operate, they'd take her to Seaview and make her live there, *oh my God...*

She needed to punch the Communicaid. It was on the hook near the toilet, down by her feet. She tried to move and the pain was so great she uttered a cry and fell back.

She lay there gasping, clammy, shaky. *Rest for a minute, rest.*

She closed her eyes. She thought: *Thank God for the oil heat, I'd never be able to feed the woodstove, not like this.*

Her hip began to ease a bit, now throbbed with a deep dull ache. Her shaking stopped. *Okay, now try again.* Again bright blinding pain and a rush of sweat, but she managed to turn toward the toilet.

She inched along in agony. A swirl of dizziness, noise in her ears. At last she was under the sink.

The Communicaid was on the towel that hung above her head. She reached up as high as she could and the quick fierce jolt in her hip made her cry out loud. She dropped her arm and bit her cheek. Too high, the towel was up too high! But maybe not, her eyes played tricks. Steeling herself, she tried again. Again that agonizing pain. Too high, too high—and then the lights went out.

A line was down. No lights. It must be nearly four o'clock, and soon it would be dark. Pitch black, unless the power was restored. And cold. The furnace wouldn't run.

There were matches in the drawer of the kitchen table, candles too, but she'd never be able to reach them. There was wood in the wagon in front of the stove but she couldn't start a fire.

She reached up one more time and didn't come anywhere close to the towel, and the pain made her whimper.

She needed to get to the phone. She needed to crawl across the room to the table, grab the cord and pull down the phone and call 911.

So fast, it had happened so fast, that's what Gerald had said. An oily spot on the floor of the mill and he slipped and the saw took two fingers and sliced through his lung. So fast that he didn't know what had happened. At first there had been no pain. He'd looked at his hand without understanding, then pain and he'd gone into shock.

It was already getting cold in the bathroom. No air was coming out of the duct by the flush.

She'd been right after all about her stove, her Home Comfort. She wouldn't be able to feed it, no, but its heat would die slowly, last for hours, not like this foolish furnace. She'd gone through power outages that lasted days when she had the Home Comfort going.

Days! She'd never survive the night without heat. *Dear God let the power come on!*

She still lay on the broken hip. To make it across the room she would need to turn over. She pushed and pushed and raised herself and the pain was astounding. She let herself down again. Took a breath.

She couldn't believe the intensity of the pain. Her ears were shot, her eyes were shot, her fingertips were numb, yet her flesh was as sensitive as ever. How could that be?

She balled her gnarled hands into fists. *Try again!* This pain wasn't any worse than when Bobby was born and she tore her insides apart. No worse than that—but then she'd been twenty years old.

Again she pushed, cried out, pushed on, pushed through it, managed to turn herself over. Lay gasping.

She shivered. Cold, it was getting cold fast, and getting dark. She inched forward. Better, not as much pain.

Her arm hit the threshold. Oak. Gerald had made it. Gerald had built the bathroom after the war; before that they had a backhouse out in the shed. Gerald could make almost anything out of wood, could fix all kinds of machines—machines that sat in the barn now rusting away. She herself had made trousers and shirts and dresses; had knitted mittens and hats, had crocheted doilies and tablecloths. Had tended the garden and cooked and canned and put up preserves. Won prizes for years at the Paradise Fair for her blueberry pies. Then after Gerald died, she cleaned houses for people. Now all that was gone, she couldn't do anything now.

And maybe this fall was a message from God, telling her she should die. What good was she now to anyone? No good at all.

We'll manage, she said to Gerald. *We got through Bobby's death and we'll get through this. You'll get your strength back, I know you will, and someday we'll go on our journey.* He nodded, pale in the big maple bed. The sight of the stumps where his fingers had been turned her stomach. *Wilma,* he said, *I'd be lost without you.*

He tried, he tried, but losing that lung and those fingers had done something to him. He still worked hard, but it took so much effort. He tired quickly and much of the time he seemed lost in his thoughts. He started to take down terrible bad, and one day he didn't wake up.

Wilma's head was now touching the threshold. She thought: *For God's sake, what are you doing? Why are you thinking about all that? You have to get to the phone.*

She hooked her arm over the threshold and pulled, jaw tight. Gerald said, *You're a strong woman, Wilma, don't know none stronger.* She pulled and her pelvis struck the thick ridge of oak. The pain!

He did what he had to do. He fought for our country, he was a hero.

I know, I know, but it doesn't matter, I just want him back. My Bobby, I want him back. Thank God Frank has that problem with his eyes or he'd of gone in too. I want my little boy, my strong young man, I want my Bobby...

Bobby?

Nobody here but her, she was down on the floor. On the floor, for a minute she'd thought she heard Bobby. She let out a breath.

The phone. Over there on the table, all the way over there. They said she should have a second one for the nightstand next to the bed, but two phones in one room seemed foolish. Nobody called but the nurses or credit card people. Most of the day she sat at the table. If somebody called when she was in bed, she let it go. If she'd listened to what Community Action said and got that second phone it would be in her hand right now.

The floor shivered under her. Only did that when the wind was real strong. *Big storm. Must be. The power line down. Could they get up the road?*

Frank, why did you try to drive up the road in this ice?

I thought I could make it before it got really bad.

Now look what you've done to your truck.

I hate this damn weather! I hate this goddamn place, this goddamn state!

Lung cancer in California. Gerald dead and she flew there with Charlotte. First and only time on a plane. Frank looking like something out of a concentration camp, big oxygen tank near his bed, tubes in his nose. No wife to comfort him, he'd never married. Wilma had held back her tears to give him strength.

You're a strong woman.

Why did you have to go, Bobby?

Where was she? Dark, so dark, was she down on the floor? *Have to get myself up, why...? Oh, I remember now...*

She pulled herself forward. Her shoulder hit something. Her walker. She pushed it aside.

The floor trembled again. Cold, terribly cold, the wind had sucked all the heat right out of the house and she needed Olive. *Olive, come over here, keep me warm. Where are you, come on, be a good dog now...*

No, don't you remember, Wilma? Olive's dead. But Annie, I thought you told me...

Annie? Who's Annie? Why had she thought that? *I need to get to the phone.*

She pulled herself forward again. *What's this?*

Wagon. Bobby's red wagon.

Bobby you left your wagon out on the floor, why...?

Don't worry now, Mama, I'll be just fine.

His uniform, handsome, she held him kissed him. Eyes so blue. Nineteen years old. His bones in a coffin, sent by airplane, all that was left. Killed in action, fierce fighting. Bobby who'd never fought anyone in his life, who'd been so good to the animals...

He's a hero, Wilma.

Gerald's voice calm and strong and his arm around her. And then when she went to the shed for the wood she heard a strange noise in the barn and in one of the stalls out of sight it was Gerald, weeping.

Words and images racing around in her head in the dark. *Bobby.* Pulled herself forward, felt the hearth. Not far from the door. No life in her shoulders and neck, so terribly cold and the pain in her hip. She pushed.

The leg of the table. Yes. Inched forward, and now her chair. The phone cord under here somewhere. *Where is it? Has to be here...*

This was it? Could hardly feel it. Yes. She pulled.

The phone came crashing down right in front of her face.

Receiver, got it, pressed it to her ear.

No sound.

She always heard the dial tone when she held the phone to her ear, she wasn't as deaf as all that. But now no sound.

The line was dead. Electric and phone both out. Of course.

She took a deep breath, exhaled. The air felt wet. So cold. Too cold, she was going to die.

Well all right, then. Everyone else was dead so all right.

She lay there, breathing cold, her shoulders and right arm numb. Right here on the floor and who lost his hat? Was it Gerald or Frank? *Frank, did you lose your hat?*

No, no, can't dream you dream you die! But everyone else is dead. Now Charlotte too after all those years when she didn't know who you were saw things not there a waking dream...

A pressure in her bladder, sudden, strong. That's how it happened now, so fast. Often she barely made it into the bathroom.

No. Just went not long ago before you fell how long ago so cold...

Squeezing her eyes shut and gritting her teeth, she swung away from the table. Sudden sharp pain in her hip, and then, with a cry, she let go.

Warmth down her leg, the only warmth. She lay there breathing hard.

She'd never wet herself before, never in all her life. That's what they put you in Seaview for, for wetting yourself. A rush of shame.

No, no, you couldn't help it, Gerald said.

He was there by the stove. *Gerald? What are you doing down here? You ought to be resting, up in bed.*

I'm writing from Belgium, Mama.

Belgium. She'd never been out of Maine, not even to Massachusetts. California many years later when Frank took sick.

Bobby why did you go so far away? So far away to die?

The pain of Bobby's birth had lasted three long days, but the pain of his dying had never stopped.

Leg wet, all wet, now cold, and music somewhere. *Bed warm, crawl back pull the covers down. Across the room.*

Soft music. Wind?

We've always been here, Wilma, you know that, we never left.

So this was how you served the Lord: by never giving up.

We never left.

I know that, Gerald, felt you in the garden with me, felt you in the shed. Felt Bobby when I pulled his wagon Frank was there when I called maple under...

No! Not that! Not taken watch can't who...

She sighed, and suddenly so blue, so intensely, incredibly blue. Why had she never noticed before how blue it was right here? And opened up into a meadow with Indian paintbrush daisies. Wasn't that Bobby? Warm she was floating above the ground.

Our journey, Wilma.

But where did you get the money? How did you get so young? Look at your hand it's healed you have all your fingers.

A place so grand you can't believe.

And Bobby too?

Of course.

It's blue we're warm, oh Gerald I'm so happy now. Sky blue so blue I never saw such blue inside me breathing blue...

You'll come before. To bring down cellar more from summer run again by time with carrots maybe force same dark if blood some tree rain which barn over catch less doorway whisper take low hard now light...car...bird...

～

"Mrs. Potter?"

Blurred movement. Bright so heavy. Oh.

"You fell asleep again. Can you hear me?"

Nodding, slightly, head so heavy. "Room am I in?" Her voice a weak dry croak.

"You're in the hospital."

"What?"

"YOU'RE IN THE HOSPITAL, MRS. POTTER."

"Oh." Not dead. She wasn't dead.

"How are you feeling?"

"What?"

"YOU FEEL OKAY?"

"I'm tired."

"I guess you are. Do you know who I am?"

"No."

"Annie, the nurse who came to see you yesterday."

"Did you say Annie?"

"Yes."

"Oh, Annie." She remembered.

"The power was going out all over the place and I was concerned about you. I called, but didn't get any ring and the phone sounded funny. I figured your lines were down and called 911. They found you on the floor beside your bed unconscious."

"You called me?"

"Yes."

"Oh. That was nice." And now the pain again, far off, as if at the end of a tunnel. "I broke my hip."

"You did. Your house was freezing, and your temperature had dropped real low. You'd left your Communicaid in the bathroom and couldn't call for help and your phone was on the floor and off the hook. It was a close one, Mrs. Potter, but now you're going to be fine."

"Fine," Wilma said.

"Once you get strong enough, they'll replace your hip, then take you to Seaview for rehab."

"What?"

"YOU'LL GO TO SEAVIEW FOR REHAB."

"Seaview."

"For rehab, not to stay."

"No."

"How's your hip? I can get them to give you some more medication."

"It's not that bad."

"You're strong, Mrs. Potter."

"It just doesn't hurt that much right now. I guess it's what they're giving me."

"It's powerful stuff."

"I guess. So did you go?"

"Go where?"

"To Florida."

"Oh, no, Mrs. Potter, that's not till next week."

"Oh? Oh, next week. I got my times mixed up."

The blur that was Annie stood and said, "That's no surprise, with all that you've been through. Well look, I know you're very tired, I'm going to let you rest."

"What's that?"

"I'M GOING TO LET YOU REST."

"God bless you, dear."

"God bless you, too,"

"I hope you have a real nice trip."

"Thanks, Mrs. Potter. Rest up now."

"I will."

The blur moved off and Wilma sighed, then closed her eyes on memories of blue.

Holly Point

Richard had hoped to arrive at the camp before sunset, and now it was almost dark. He guided the wagon into the slot by the side of the lane, killed the engine and lights, then just sat for a minute, breathing the clean cool air through the open window. Out in the field that spread to the black line of trees, a cricket chirped.

Mark took off his seat belt, opened his door, and went to the back of the wagon. Richard joined him. The dome light shone on his hands as he said, "Let's try to remember everything. You have the toilet kit?"

"I'm getting it."

"The radio?"

"You think I'd forget the radio?"

Mark had turned twelve a month ago; his passion for music knew no bounds.

"Sleeping bags, toilet kit, radio, food, doors locked," Richard said as he turned on the flashlight. "Okay, let's go. And watch your step."

"Yeah, Dad," Mark said.

Their running shoes made crunching sounds on the dark sloping gravel lane. The flashlight's beam struck rocks and roots. A bat darted into the channel of inky blue above their heads, dead black and jittery, then disappeared. Straight up, a single star. Soon, on the beach, the sky would be filled with stars.

"Looks like it might be a cool one," Richard said.

"It's always a cool one at Holly Point," Mark said.

The camp belonged to Donald James, an accountant Richard had met on the Limerock tennis courts six years ago. It sat on the shore behind granite slabs, on the edge of a forest of spruce. Don had invited Richard there for a drink once after a tennis game. When Richard told him how much he admired the place, Don surprised him by saying, "You're welcome to use it. We only get down here a couple of weeks all season, just give me a call." It was one of those generous, trusting Maine gestures that even now—after a dozen summers on the coast—Richard found hard to believe.

Before heading back to New Jersey that year, he'd taken Don up on his offer. Joan didn't like camping out, so she stayed with a friend while her "boys" went to Holly Point one spectacular afternoon, swam in the ocean, cooked on the outdoor granite fireplace, slept on the sandy beach. Ever since, Mark and Richard had ended their summers that way.

When Richard returned the key the third summer, he asked Don James if land at the Point was for sale. Frowning and looking away at the houses across from the tennis courts, Don answered, "Not that I know of, no land for sale down there in years," and Richard had never asked the question again.

That winter, Mark's headaches began. He was stuck with a teacher he couldn't stand, his best friend moved to Washington, he was cut from the basketball team—any or all or none of which might have brought on the headaches, which came every month or so. They announced themselves with a pain in the eye that grew till it claimed the entire right side of his head. He would quiver all over and rock back and forth on the edge of his bed, moaning. After an hour or so of this he would vomit hard and sleep for half a day.

The pediatrician couldn't help and suggested a psychotherapist, who wired Mark's index finger and forehead, then had him lean back in a leather recliner. "Picture a calm and peaceful place, a place where you're safe," he said in a baritone drone. "See yourself lying there, comfortable, warm." Mark's eyelids closed; his hands went limp. Richard had never seen him look so relaxed, and he found himself drifting off too.

On the way home he asked, "What place did you think of?"

Mark looked at him. "Holly Point."

Richard smiled. "Me too."

After six sessions, Mark had become an expert at stopping his headaches. And Richard, at work, would lean back in his swivel chair, think of the cabin, the sky, the trees, the slow rub of water on pebbles and sand, and return to his task refreshed. "The Holly Point Cure," he called it.

~

And now, as he walked down the rutted lane, he was struck by a wave of excitement: for soon he would have a place of his own down here. After their first tennis session this year, Don James said, "Still looking for land?"

Richard said that he was.

"I own a small piece to the east of my camp," Don said. "The road down there's a little rough, but passable. Nice spot."

The very next day, Richard looked at the land and put a down payment on it.

"How's it going?" he said to Mark, who was lagging behind. "Want to rest?"

This was the first time he'd traveled the lane in the dark and he wasn't sure where he was. The fork should be coming up soon—or maybe they'd passed it.

Mark shifted his load. "Let's keep going," he said, and a sad bird suddenly started to sing in the depths of the evening trees. "We can't camp on our land tonight," Mark said. "It's too dark and we won't be able to find a good spot."

"I know," Richard said.

"Well how come you stopped at Jeannie and Bill's?"

"I wanted to say goodbye. I won't see them again till next summer."

"Okay, but such a *long* goodbye."

"I'm sorry," Richard said.

Just the song of the bird and the scuff of their feet, and then Mark said, "What's that?"

"What?"

"Stop."

And now Richard could hear it: an engine coughing, straining, dying. Then out of the darkness a husky voice snarled, "Shit!"

Dead quiet, not even the bird. Then Richard started to walk again, his light pointed down, and Mark followed.

The pickup was parked at the fork. They didn't see the man at the wheel until they were right up close. His features were lost in darkness. Long hair...

"What happened, you run out of gas?" Richard said.

No reply. Then the man tipped his head back. "Yeah."

"I think I can get you some," Richard said.

The dark shadow leaned forward. The engine fought and fought and fought and quit. The man banged the steering wheel hard with the flat of his hand.

"I'll be back in a couple of minutes," Richard said.

No reply from the truck.

"Mark?"

They went down the lane to the cabin and put all their stuff on the porch, and Richard told Mark to wait while he went out back.

As always, the door to the shed was unlocked. The flashlight beam fell on the red can of gas that Don kept for his mower and boat. Richard lifted it up. Almost empty. He went with it back to the cabin.

"I want to come with you," Mark said.

Richard didn't reply for a moment, then said, "Okay, take the light."

When they reached the truck, Richard said to its driver, "I got it."

Again, no response. The man was invisible now in the night. Richard went to the back of the truck; unscrewed the gas cap as Mark held the light; unscrewed the cap on the gasoline spout and poured the can's contents into the tank. When the flashlight tipped upward its light shined on clam hods, most of them empty.

"Okay," Richard said to the man. "Try again."

The engine turned over, then suddenly sputtered and caught. Dirt and stones flew away from the wheels as the truck shot out. Gears rang and its lights came on; one taillight was dead and the other was shaky and dim.

"Didn't even say thanks," Mark said as the truck disappeared.

"Let's be happy he's gone," Richard said.

They walked down the lane to the cabin again. As Richard put the gas can back in the shed he said, "Remind me to get this filled before we leave."

They went back to the porch, and Mark shined the light on the door. "Oh jeez," he said.

One of the door's glass panes had been smashed.

"He was breaking in," Richard said.

"And he stopped when he heard us coming. We chased him away."

"Yeah—and helped him escape."

"We should call the police," Mark said.

"There's no phone down here."

"Oh, right."

"We'll call tomorrow."

They went inside. Richard turned on the light and the place looked the same. Year after year, it was always the same: same furniture, same braided rug over green painted floor, same waterstained pine plank walls. The sameness was one of the things Richard loved about it.

He went to a window, opened it, and heard the soft wash of the sea.

Mark said, "I'm starving."

"Let's eat," Richard said.

Outside again, they gathered twigs and got a fire going. The fireplace crackled; sparks flew to the sky. They threaded their hot dogs on freshly cut pin cherry branches and blistered and blackened them, toasted some marshmallows for dessert. They spread out the coals and went to the cabin and got their sleeping bags.

"Why doesn't Don lock his shed?" Mark asked as they walked back down to the beach.

"Most people just don't around here."

"Just think if we left our garage in New Jersey unlocked."

Richard laughed.

Thirty feet down from the granite slabs they spread out their sleeping bags, then walked to the water's edge. The crescent moon gave little light, but plenty enough to see the craters left by a clamdigger's fork.

"Would you look at this mess," Richard said.

Yards and yards of beach had been overturned, and here and there the side of a beer bottle caught the pale light. Richard gathered the bottles, five in all. Tire tracks led from the clamming site, and the tide had discovered them, sending small rivulets into their grooves. Pretty soon they'd be gone.

"Well, I'm ready for bed," Richard said.

"Me too," Mark said.

They went back up the beach, Richard holding the bottles. A gentle breeze came from the east. *From my land,* Richard thought. *This breeze is coming from my land.*

Without getting undressed they slid into their sleeping bags. As usual, no insects here. Soon Mark was breathing rhythmically. In that terrible stretch when he'd had his migraines, he'd frequently taken hours to fall asleep.

Richard looked at the stars. Three more days and vacation would end. By Sunday afternoon they'd be back in New Jersey—hot crowded polluted New Jersey, the Garden State. He and Joan would go back to their jobs and Mark would go back to school, and another ten months would pass before they'd return to Maine. But now they owned land here and someday, somehow, they would move here for good.

He stared at the infinite splash of stars, the air now cool and deep with the smell of the sea. Below, the gentle surf advanced, erasing the hills of sand and mud left behind by the clamdigger, soothing and healing. His eyelids closed.

~

The engine woke him an instant before he heard Mark holler, "Dad!" and he spun around to see headlights coming straight at him. Completely confused, completely awake, he thought: *We're dead!* Then the vehicle stopped about fifty feet off, made a wild wide turn and went back up the beach.

"It's that man!" Mark said.

He was right: one taillight was feeble, the other was black.

The engine revved and the headlights were on them again.

"Dad!"

"Stay still!" Richard said, and his heartbeat was painful, huge.

The truck rushed up closer this time before braking. It idled a moment, then turned.

"It's a game," Richard said.

"Dad, I'm scared!"

"Yeah, that's just what he wants."

"He's coming again!"

"Just stay still," Richard said. "If we get up and run now, he'll chase us."

"But Dad!"

"Stay still!"

The truck roared up out of the east again, out of the land that was now Richard's land, its lights on high beam. It braked, skidding sideways and spewing sand, and sat with its engine growling. It started to make its turn and Richard said, "Okay! Let's go!"

They raced across the sand to the granite slabs. The truck spun around and its headlights splashed over their arms, their hands.

"Run!" Richard said.

They reached the rocks, climbed over them, crouching

down. The pickup braked and its lights hit the cabin. A creak of hinges, a string of curses, a shatter of glass on the rocks. Then the slam of the door, the lights in a wide sweeping arc on the sand and the truck was gone.

It was quiet again. Dark. Stars.

"I'm hurt," Mark said.

They went into the cabin. Blood oozed from a gash on Mark's left shin. His chest was heaving as he said, "He tried to kill us."

"No, just scare us," Richard said.

"But why? We gave him gas."

"I don't know why. Let's fix you up."

He took a clean towel from the cabinet beside the sink, ran water on it, washed the wound. Mark winced, but didn't cry. Richard tied a different towel, a dishtowel, over the cut and said, "That'll do till tomorrow."

"I want to go home," Mark said.

"We can't, not now," Richard said. "That lane would be murder on your leg."

"But what if the man comes back?"

"He won't. He's had his fun."

Richard went to the beach for the sleeping bags. The sea's methodical push, vast sky, bright stars—as if nothing had happened. In the cabin he spread the bags out on the floor.

"I can't sleep here," Mark said.

"Mark—"

"Dad, I can't."

They left their things in the cabin and started out. "If he comes—" Mark said.

"He won't," Richard said. Then, softening his tone, he said, "How's your leg?"

"Not too bad, but my eye—"

"What about it?"

"It hurts."

By the time they reached the station wagon, Mark's whole body was shaking. They got inside. "Let's go," Mark said with a desperate edge to his voice, "let's get out of this place." His right hand was pressed to his forehead.

Richard turned the key and the engine struggled. He pumped the accelerator. "Now what?" he said. "Come on."

Then he noticed the gas gauge. "Jesus Christ, he siphoned our tank! And the can down at Don's is empty."

"I'm having a migraine," Mark said in a whimper. "I'm going to be sick."

Richard turned to him. "Try to relax. Just close your eyes and—"

Thrusting himself at the window, Mark retched. He hung there, groaning. Heaved again, breathed hard and slumped back in his seat.

"It's over," Richard said. "That's it, you're okay now."

"I'm not," Mark said with his hands on his face. "I'm not okay, it's changed here now. It's different now."

The dark closed in, a cricket rasped, Richard thought of the therapist's words: *Picture a calm and peaceful place, a place where you're safe...*

"I'm not okay, I'm not," Mark said again, and this time he wept.

Home

As they entered the turnpike a tractor trailer rushed up behind them, its headlights huge and menacing. Their old Toyota fought with the grade and the truck stayed right on their tail, pushing and pushing and Allen said, "Damn it! They're high on speed and they play these games at four o'clock in the morning!"

"We should have left later," Rachel said. "You know you always hate to drive in the dark."

"It's a twelve hour trip," Allen said. "At *least* twelve hours. We've never done it before and we'll probably get lost."

"I hope not."

"Come on, man, get off me!"

Nathan, their ten month old, was strapped in his safety seat in the back. He was wide awake.

Allen's knuckles were tight on the wheel. The Toyota would go no faster. "A baby in back, and he drives this close," he said.

Rachel looked in her side view mirror. "Forget him," she said, "he's not going to hit us."

"Oh? What if we have to stop real fast?"

"Don't think about that."

A space opened up on the left. The truck cut away with a blare of its horn and pursued a blue Chevy.

"Nice guy," Allen said.

Ten minutes later a band of gray appeared in the east over flat long industrial buildings. "Cloudy," Rachel said. "Well, that was the forecast."

Soon a light drizzle began, then rain.

~

The Garden State Parkway below New York was a tangle, bumper to bumper in spots with incredible lines at the toll-booths. The rain was steady and Nathan was fussing and Rachel gave him a biscuit to quiet him down. The Tappan Zee Bridge was clotted with traffic, the rain came harder, they almost missed the turn for New England. "Yeah, wouldn't that have been something?" Allen said. "Already an hour behind."

In Connecticut they stopped for gas and to change Nathan's diaper. Back on the road they ate apples and cheese and the rain continued. "We'll stop for lunch, won't we?" Rachel asked. "We can't just eat snacks."

They ate at McDonald's in Massachusetts and took a wrong turn getting back on the road. This cost them twenty minutes. The rain had let up for a while but now it was starting again. By the time they reached the Maine state line they'd been driving eleven hours.

After the tollbooth, running his rain-damp hand through his curly hair, Allen said, "Another two hours to go."

"Let's stay over someplace," Rachel said.

"The woman's expecting us."

"You have her number?"

"No."

"You didn't bring her *number?*"

"She didn't *give* it to me," Allen said.

"We'll call directory assistance then."

"It's only four fifteen, let's just keep going."

"I'm so *tired,*" Rachel said.

"Me too, but we can make it."

"God, this *rain*. It's a *cold* rain, too."

"What was it, ninety yesterday at home?"

"At least. The sign on that bank we just passed said fifty-eight."

"Wow. At the end of *June.*"

Rachel was quiet a moment then said, "I hope this isn't a mistake."

"It's not."

"You didn't *have* to come."

"They've asked me to for three years now."

"You didn't *have* to, though."

"I just want to see what the summer program's like—and what Maine's like. They pay for our cottage, so how can we lose?"

"We can lose if someone breaks into our house," Rachel said. "I mean leaving it empty for two whole months..."

"The house'll be fine. Bob'll check on it every week."

"A lot can happen in a week."

"It won't," Allen said.

The rain would not let up and the light was fading. Two hours later, starving and weary, they stopped at a diner—"EAT" said a red neon sign with a moving arrow pointing down—and sat in a brown vinyl booth. The walls of the place were a pale mint green. A burly waitress arrived with menus and spoke in an accent that made them smile. When she came back to take their order she said, "He's just so cunnin'."

A reference to Nathan. They didn't know how to respond.

"How old is he?" the waitress asked.

"Ten months," Rachel said.

"So cunnin', yes you are." A big wide grin. "You need more time or you all set?"

"The mashed potatoes," Rachel said. "Are they real?"

"Everything here is real," the waitress said, still smiling at Nathan.

After she left again Allen said, "Cunning? *Smart?*"

"It must mean something else," Rachel said. "Cute or something."

"Looks like we're going to need language lessons," Allen said.

The food was good and plentiful and boosted their spirits. The bill was amazingly small. The cashier smiled and said, "Thank you much, you have a good evenin' now." She sounded like she meant it.

"Good choice," Allen said as they went through the door to the cold unceasing rain.

In the car he checked the map. "Only twenty more miles."

"Thank God," Rachel said.

It seemed farther than that. Trees, mostly evergreens, lining the road, and not much else, and now it was getting dark.

"What a desolate place," Rachel said.

"The rain makes it seem that way," Allen said.

"It *is* that way."

Luckily, they had no trouble finding the woman's house; her directions had been precise. A light was on at the side of the place. Allen pulled into the driveway behind an old Dodge sedan; got out, went up the steps, and rang the bell.

The door opened quickly.

"You have to be Mr. Miller," the woman said. She was round-faced and ruddy, with thick white hair.

"Mrs. Briggs," Allen said.

"Come in."

He stepped inside. An old fashioned kitchen: tall wooden cabinets, old stove and fridge, a sink made out of slate.

"You must be exhausted," Mrs. Briggs said. "You've eaten, I hope."

"We stopped at that diner on Route One."

"Oh good. Well you probably want to get right on down there, what with the baby. How is he?"

"Fine."

"That's good to hear."

Mrs. Briggs put a rain hat and jacket on and they went out again. "It's not too far," she said. "Oh isn't this weather awful." She waved at Rachel then started the Dodge and Allen backed up to let her out. He followed her through the town.

They went down a street of Victorian houses and past a corner with fire house, gas station, Dairy Queen. They rattled across some railroad tracks. More houses, smaller, hard to see in the steady rain. They followed the big car's taillights left, then right, through a long stretch of nothing but trees. Mrs. Briggs put her turn signal on and slowed and went left again on an unpaved road. It was quite dark now. Just trees as they bumped along.

"No street lights at all," Rachel said. "We're *nowhere*."

The Dodge made another right turn, and after a minute it stopped.

"Home sweet home, I guess," Rachel said.

Their headlights shone on the trunk of the big old car. Mrs. Briggs got out and came up to the window. "You pull around into that space over there, you'll be out of my way."

Allen backed the Toyota into the slot. By the time he finished, a light was on in the cottage.

"Well isn't this simply awful," Mrs. Briggs said when they came inside. "Supposed to clear off by tomorrow, though. Let's hope so, we need the tourists." She smiled at Nathan. "Hello there, sweetie. You must be *wicked* tired."

She showed them the oil stove in the kitchen. "Let's hope you won't have to use this much. It's on right now because of the damp." She taught them how to regulate it, light it, turn it off. "You have any problems, let me know, I'm home all day tomorrow."

Crossing to the door, she said, "Now here's the key." It hung on a nail beside the jamb. "You won't need it, of course, nobody locks things here. My number's on that yellow card, police and fire too. Feel free to call me anytime."

"Thanks," Allen said.

Mrs. Briggs frowned, "This door's been sticking, I hope it won't give you trouble. I'll get someone out here to fix it as soon as I can. I'll leave you alone now. Enjoy your cake."

When the Dodge was gone, Rachel said, "Our cake?"

It was there on the kitchen table. "Looks like banana bread," Allen said. "How nice of her."

"Very nice," Rachel said. Nathan squirmed in her arms. "Allen, what are we *doing* here?"

"Let's put Nathan to bed. We should think about sleeping too."

"There won't be anything *else* to do in a place like this. We are *nowhere*."

"I like being nowhere," Allen said.

The downstairs was basically one big room with the kitchen along one wall. A couple of rocking chairs and a couch sat in front of a large stone fireplace. Glass doors led to a sunporch; beyond that, a deck. The walls were dark unfinished wood, and so was the floor. Copper water pipes followed the rafters, as did the wiring. "Quaint," Rachel said.

They went up the narrow, twisting stairs and put Nathan into the crib in the tiny room to the right of the tiny bathroom. The toilet roared when they pulled the chain. They undressed and got into bed—an antique white iron thing with jiggly springs. Allen tugged on the cord above his head and the ceiling light went out.

It was dark: really dark, pitch black. Rain drummed on the slanted boards above their heads. "Do I need sleep," Allen said.

"It's so *lonely* here," Rachel said as she curled up beside him. "I already miss the city."

"We'll adapt," Allen said.

"I hope so. The people, they're so...so *country*."

"Pleasant, though."

"Pleasant isn't enough."

"You'll get used to them," Allen said.

"Do I want to? Now what's that noise?"

"What noise?"

"That moaning sound. You hear it?"

Allen listened. "That?"

"Uh-huh."

"A foghorn. There must be a lighthouse around here some-where."

"Oh."

Allen was starting to drift away when he suddenly snapped awake. "Oh no," he said, and Rachel said, "What now?"

"The car. I forgot to lock it."

"You didn't."

"I did."

"Well you're not going out there now."

"Of course I am."

"Mrs. Briggs said that people don't lock things here."

"All our stuff's in the car," Allen said, "I can't take the chance." He turned on the light again, put on his clothes, and went down the stairs.

He came back soaked.

Rachel said, "Did you lock the door?"

"Of course."

"Well don't say 'Of course'—you left the car open."

"Hey, give me a break."

~

They woke to the sound of Nathan babbling. The white-curtained window was bright and the foghorn had stopped. Rachel got out of bed. The floorboards were cold and she shivered. She crossed the hall.

Nathan greeted her with a smile. She lifted him out of the crib and said, "Morning, honey, you sleep all right?" then she looked at the window. "My God," she said.

Rugged boulders, a thin stretch of sand and the water, so vast, stretching out to dark islands and shimmering, dancing with sun. "Allen, look," she called.

He came into the room. "Wow," he said. "Incredible."

"I've never seen anything like it."

"Me neither."

"And there's the lighthouse, out on that island."

"Yes, there it is."

They put on their clothes and fed Nathan out on the sunporch, which was warm. Outside, mist rose from the deck.

"Irises," Rachel said. "Ours were finished a month ago. Oh, look!"

"Now *that's* a hummingbird," Allen said. "Gigantic! Look, Nathan."

The child's head turned.

"It's gone," Rachel said.

"They don't hang around very long."

Rachel looked at the water, the islands. "The light on those *trees,*" she said.

They ate some cake, then put all their stuff in the cottage and locked the door and drove up the narrow lane. They saw other cottages now, invisible the night before, scattered among the trees along the shore. As they made the turn onto the wider road, the bay spread before them again in a crisp bright arc. "I'm impressed," Allen said.

A car came down the road on the opposite side. As it passed them, the driver, a middleaged man, took a hand off the wheel and waved.

"Who was that?" Rachel asked.

"I don't know."

"Not somebody from the school?"

"Could be. I couldn't see him well."

"Good thing you waved back."

On their right, the trees opened into a meadow with thousands of flowers: yellow and orange on slender stalks, and daisies, brilliant white.

"I've never seen daisies that huge before," Rachel said.

"It's a children's book illustration," Allen said. "Fantastic!"

Another car went by and again a wave.

"Maybe people just do that here," Allen said.

"They'll know at the school, I guess."

They parked on Main Street and ate at a place called "The Coffee Shop." It equaled the diner in quality, price and decor. The waitress asked them how long they would be in Maine.

In the car again Allen said, "I don't think we're going to pass for natives."

"Not unless we get that accent down," Rachel said. "That waitress—when she said, 'Yeah," she breathed *in*."

"I noticed that."

Rachel gave it a try. "God, how do they do it? I'd choke to death if I talked that way."

They shopped at a small supermarket. The prices were higher than in the city and no one was in a hurry, especially the cashiers.

"I thought we'd never get out of there," Rachel said as they drove off again. "There must be a bigger store somewhere."

"Maybe not," Allen said. "Maybe not nearby."

"Are you going out to the school?"

"On Saturday? Ross won't even be there. I'll give them a call to tell them I'm here and report on Monday."

"Good idea."

"Is this the street we were on last night?"

"You're asking me?"

"Nice houses," Allen said.

Huge Victorians, mostly white, and mostly in good repair, with hedges and flowers and closely trimmed lawns.

"Uh-oh," Allen said.

"What?"

"You smell gas?"

"Yeah. Is that us?"

He pulled to the side of the road, popped the hood and got out. When he came back he said, "Carburetor. It's leaking."

"Great, just what we need."

"If we're on the same street we were on last night, there's a gas station up ahead."

They were on the same street. Allen stopped at the station. In the open garage, a mechanic in dark blue coveralls was leaning over a Buick's engine. He didn't look up as Allen approached.

Not wanting to ruin the man's concentration, Allen just stood there. Finally the man said, "Yessah."

Clearing his throat, Allen said, "I have a carburetor leak, could you possibly look at it?"

The man straightened up. His face was lined and tufts of gray stuck out from under a Red Sox cap. Without a word, he went to the Toyota.

Allen opened the hood and the man looked around. "Yessah," he said again, went back to the garage, returned with some tools. He bent down and worked for a couple of minutes. "That oughta do it," he said.

"It's fixed?" Allen said.

"Oughta be. If she gives you more trouble you bring 'er back."

"Well...okay. How much do I owe you?"

The man shook his head.

"Well I must owe you *something*."

"Nope."

"Well...thanks," Allen said.

In the car, Rachel said, "What's the story?"

"He fixed it. For nothing."

"For *nothing?*"

"For nothing—and *instantly*. In the city I'd have to make an appointment and leave it all day."

"Incredible. We'll have to buy our gas from him."

"We will indeed."

While Nathan took his post-lunch nap, they read the *New York Times* they had bought in town. Allen gave the school a call, and when Nathan woke up, they went for a walk on the beach. It was narrow and rocky, with small sandy stretches, and tiny, gentle waves.

Rachel tested the water. "My God," she said, "I bet it's not even sixty."

The boulders lining the bank were covered with gray and gold lichen, and so were the small spruce trees. Every so often, a small tidepool in the rocks: clear shallow water with tiny mussels and shrimp, a miniature world.

~

They slept well that night, but Allen woke up with a backache, the aftermath of unloading the car. They went into town for the Sunday *Times*. When they returned, the telephone rang. In the quiet, it startled them.

It was Mrs. Briggs. Could someone stop by to work on the kitchen door? She didn't want to disturb their Sunday, but Mr. Hobbs had some time today. Allen said fine—and thanks for the cake.

Mr. Hobbs was stocky, fifty or so, with thin red hair. He examined the door and said, "Have to redo a bit of this frame, it might take a while."

"No problem," Allen said. "If you need us, we'll be on the deck."

At one point, Rachel went inside to get some juice for Nathan. "I heard that man say the strangest thing," she said when she came back.

"To himself?" Allen said.

"To himself. He's having some problems with the job, I guess, and he said, 'Oh dear.'"

"'Oh *dear?*"

Rachel grinned. "Not quite what carpenters at home would say."

A short while later, Allen went in for some water, and Mr. Hobbs was packing up his tools. "Well, that oughta be a whole lot better," he said. "That frame was some crooked." He squinted. "You hurt your back?"

Allen smiled a little. "How'd you guess?"

"Just the way you were walkin'. I might have somethin' to help you out, let me look."

He went to his truck and returned with a bottle. "This here stuff's the best thing goin'," he said. "You get your wife to rub you down real good before bed then again in the mornin'. Couple of days you'll be like new."

Allen took the white bottle. "Well thanks," he said. "How much does it cost?"

"Oh, I have more, you don't need to pay me."

"You sure, I—"

"You don't need to pay me. Now listen, this door gives you problems, you tell Mrs. Briggs an' I'll be right back."

"Okay. Thanks again."

"The lock's kinda stiff, but I guess you don't use that anyway."

"No," Allen said.

~

Rachel would drive Allen down the dirt road to the school every weekday morning, then pick him up again in the late afternoon. For a week she simply relaxed at the cottage, sitting on the deck with Nathan, drinking tea and reading and looking out over the water. The weather was spectacular: thin fog in the morning, followed by brilliant blue with towering clouds, the light on the islands hypnotizing, endlessly absorbing. By the start of the second week Rachel was sketching, and soon after that she was painting.

Allen remarked on the change in her style.

"You like it," she said.

"I think it's great."

"I'm excited."

"That picture just jumps off the canvas."

"I never saw light like this before. Even the fog is different here. Everything's *made* of light."

~

Thursday afternoon of that second week, Rachel lost her wallet.

Allen had not yet gotten paid, so she cashed a personal check at a bank in town, a check for two hundred dollars. The bank hadn't asked for identification: she wrote out the check, they gave her the money, and that was that. Still finding this hard to believe, she shopped at the little supermarket, went back home, unloaded the groceries, changed and fed Nathan. It wasn't till later, while searching around for a pen in her purse, that she realized her wallet was missing.

After the sudden rush of panic, she called the supermarket. Yes, they had her wallet. She packed Nathan into the car and went to retrieve it.

She was late going after Allen, and found him walking up the school's dirt road.

He got in the car and she told him the story: "Somebody found it in the cart. I must have had it in my hand when I left the store and put it down when I picked up Nathan. A hundred and sixty dollars in there, and nobody touched it. The person who turned it in didn't leave a name. When I mentioned a reward, the guy at the store just smiled."

"Of course. He knows you're one of those crazy tourists who can't believe how things work around here."

Shifting to second, Rachel said, "It *does* take some getting used to. Smiling at strangers, waving to people on the road..."

"Well listen to *this* one," Allen said. "I was walking along here just now and a cab pulled up."

"Yeah, I saw it go by."

"The cabbie asked if I needed a ride and I thought, Cab drivers, now *they're* the same no matter where you live, always hustling up business. I told him I preferred to walk and he said, 'Just coming back from a call and thought you might need a lift.' He wanted to give me a *lift*. A free ride!"

The weather stayed good all summer. Rachel painted every day while Allen worked at the school. On weekends they'd pack a lunch and go exploring: drive down long peninsulas to villages with abandoned quarries, hayfields bordering the water, islands ringed with colorful lobster buoys. They would eat at a bench beside a pond or high on a hill with breathtaking views of the islands and bay, dozens of tiny dreamlike sailboats glittering in the sun. Once, finding themselves on an inland hill on a dirt road in brilliant noontime light, they stopped to ask a farmer for directions. "Wow," Allen said looking out to the east, "you can actually see the ocean from way up here."

The farmer replied with a deadpan face, "Yep. Never aware of that till the tourists pointed it out."

Allen blushed bright red.

~

One glorious late July Saturday morning, out on the deck drinking tea, Allen said, "I feel so *light*. I feel so *calm*."

"Me too," Rachel said. "It's the first time I've really relaxed in years."

"The quiet is just so wonderful."

"It scared me at first. It made me nervous."

"City people. Scared by quiet."

Rachel looked out at the water. "It's not real here."

"What? What do you mean?"

"It isn't the real world here. The people who live here don't know what the real world is."

"To *them* it's real."

"Well not to me. I'll need retraining when I get home— lessons in locking doors."

~

In August they found an empty house with a sale sign on it—"Harris Realtors." They parked in the dusty driveway and went out back.

The house was perched on a hill overlooking a pond. Acres of lowbush blueberries sloped to a line of tall dark trees. They picnicked there, feasting on berries, the sun high and bright in a perfect sky. "It's like heaven here," Rachel said, "completely unreal," and they came back again the next two weekends, eating their lunch and gathering berries, and Rachel painted the house from deep in the fields.

Ferry trips to the the islands, with walks along empty stone beaches. A drive down the coast to a red and white lighthouse that Rachel spent all day painting. Meals of tomatoes and string beans and corn that they bought from roadside stands with no proprietor in sight; they took what they wanted and left the correct amount, making change if they had to. "Back in the city the money box, the vegetables, the whole damn *stand* would disappear," Allen said.

The sunsets came earlier; nights turned cold. Before they knew it, they had only one week left.

$\sim$

As they sat in front of the fireplace one foggy evening, Rachel said, "I don't want to go back. I'm not ready."

"It went so fast," Allen said.

"Too fast."

"But we'll come again next year."

"Yes," Rachel said with an absent nod. She stared at the flames for a while and then, looking up, said, "I think we should move here."

He laughed.

"No, I mean it, the people are so much nicer here."

"*We're* so much nicer here."

"You're right, we are. And it's just so beautiful, so safe... Such a great place for Nathan to grow up in."

"He'd call you 'Mumma,'" Allen said.

"Mumma de-ah," Rachel said, and now it was her turn to laugh.

"Oh Rachel, we can't move here."

"Why not?"

"We just bought a house in the city. My *job's* in the city."

"I'm sure you could find a job up here. Special ed teachers can always find jobs."

"I guess. But the summers are one thing, to live here year 'round... The leaves are starting to change and it's only *August.*"

"Plenty of people live here year 'round."

"They were born here, they're used to it."

"*All* of them weren't born here," Rachel said.

Allen looked at the fire—and thought of that empty house on the hill, with the blueberry fields. He felt a quick rush of excitement. "You're serious," he said.

"I am," Rachel said.

Across the black water, out on the island, the foghorn sounded mournfully, and Allen felt suddenly sad—yet happy, too. "You're really *serious*," he said.

CHRISTOPHER FAHY

is the author of the novels *Nightflyer, Eternal Bliss, The Lyssa Syndrome* and *The Fly Must Die*. He has won the Maine Arts Commission Fiction Competition and a Grand Prize in the International Poetry Competition sponsored by Atlanta Review.